Indulge
BOOK TWO OF CRAVE SAGA

First published by Berlin DiVittore 2024

Copyright © 2024 by Berlin DiVittore

All rights reserved. No part of this publication may be reproduced, stored, or transmitted in any form or by any means, electronic, mechanical, photocopying, recording, scanning, or otherwise without written permission from the publisher. It is illegal to copy this book, post it to a website, or distribute it by any other means without permission.

This novel is entirely a work of fiction. The names, characters, and incidents portrayed in it are the work of the author's imagination. Any resemblance to actual persons, living or dead, events or localities is entirely coincidental.

Berlin DiVittore asserts the moral right to be identified as the author of this work

First Edition 2024

Indulge
Book Two of the Crave Saga

Written By
Berlin DiVittore

This book is dedicated to my wonderful parents, I have so many thanks in my heart and owe you both so much for what you have given me; but mostly I am grateful for you allowing and helping me to find my imagination and nurturing it every day, allowing it to grow.
"¡Los amaré a ambos por siempre, su Mija!"

And to my dear friend Leslie
— without whom this book may never have come into

Disclaimer:

Reader Discretion is Advised!

The themes in the following novel are of a fantasy and sensual nature. To protect the delicate minds of the impressionable and those unable to discern moral truths from fictional immorality, please abstain.

Thank you!

PROLOGUE

I feel the breeze on my face and smell the floral scent in the air. The stars sparkling above me and my only friend, the moon, shines upon my face. I hear the steady thundering gallop of my horse's hooves as I ride through the woods. I take in every moment of these small adventures for they are my only escape from the terrors of my reality. I ride without fear, without apprehension, just me and my stead. The woods are peaceful, I can hear an owl and the babbling of the nearby river as we approach. I hop to the ground allowing my horse a moment of refreshment before our dreaded return.

I sit on a nearby stone, taking out my journal and I begin to sketch the scenery before me. Finding solitude in the one place I ever felt safe. Returning to the place where I found asylum as a boy, knowing then I would do so every day henceforth. I take a deep breath as the moonlight shines down on me, and for a moment I am free.

I make the journey back to the castle, hopping off my steed as he gallops to the front entrance. The groom taking my horse to the stables as I walk briskly in through the front entrance of the castle.

"Where have you been Bastian?" my sister Angelina says as she approaches with yet another book in her hand.

"More reading, why don't you put down the books and have some experiences of your own." I jest, she says nothing just flashes a snobbish expression and retreats in the direction she had come. I chuckle at my small victory, then I ascend the stairs still grinning at the mischievous exchange only to be thwarted by the booming voice that plagues me daily.

"Sebastian!" My father shouts from above, peering down on me from the landing, "I have been searching for you everywhere."

"And by that, I am sure you mean, everyone else has been searching on your behalf, while you lie back and rest on your laurels," I say with disdain as I continue to ascend the stairs in his direction, removing my riding gloves as I walk.

"How dare you speak to me like that. I am the King!" He growls at me, standing prominently and asserting himself proudly.

"No, you are my father. Or had you forgotten?" I challenge stepping up to face him, broadening my chest and clenching my jaw. He scowls at me, neither of us spoke for there was really nowhere else to go in the dance of bravado.

Feeling just in the encounter, I retreat and strut my way around him, not getting more than a few steps away before he turns and grabs my arm.

"Release me." I rumble, giving him another sideways scowl, refusing to offer him the respect of my full eye contact.

"You listen to me, boy! I am the King and you…" He begins before he is cut off by another voice I hear daily. Only this voice I hold with great revere.

"Vladis, you unhand our son!" My mother shouts from the top of the stairs. He grimaces and cocks his jaw and slowly turns to face her.

"Patriva, must you always medal in my affairs?"

"Only when my children's well-being is at stake." She protests firmly. There is a brief pause and then he releases me with a firm push. I stumble back but my posture remains solid.

"Fine. He is your son; you deal with it." I hear my father say under his breath as he stalks off down the hall. She smiles brightly in his direction, a reflection of true regality. He scoffs at her, the echoing of his boots on the cobblestone fades as he does. I say nothing, I turn and commence my departure.

"Sebastian?" I hear my mother say. I stop, sigh, and turn to face her; to see she is now standing right behind me. "Why must you challenge your father so?"

"Why must he treat me so vile?"

"You are his only son. He... We, are all depending on you to restore the Steorra Erestés bond."

"What if I can't?" I say insecurely, my demeanor softening in my mother's presence.

"You can do anything, my little Prince. You have more love in your little finger than your father has in his whole body." She says stroking the sides of my face gently, "Your destiny is that of love, something you already possess in spades."

I give her a sideways grin and kiss the back of her hand respectfully. Then I turn to continue my retreat. Walking into my chambers, I remove my boots and garments. Then I step into a nice warm bath, just next to the window where the moon peaks in at me. I sit for a moment staring out at my old friend, remembering the solitude I had just experienced earlier in the day, thinking over my mother's words. Trying to figure out the moment my father's disposition went sour.

I gaze upon the glittering ripples of the moon's reflection dancing on the bath water until I am transported back to a moment in time. A moment that haunts me to my core. A moment when I was just a boy, my small hand gripping tightly to my fathers as he guided me down the stone stairwell. Then I hear the rattling of chains and the clanging of dungeon bars as they are slammed shut.

"What is that, Papa?" I asked in innocence and curiosity. We stop just outside the large wooden door beyond the sounds in question. He crouches down to look me in the eye.

"That is the sound of survival." He says sternly but with a trusting grin. Then after stroking my cheek with the knuckle of his index finger, he stands and opens the door. Unsure of what he means, I follow him willingly, unaware of the unspeakable nature of what lies within.

Just inside the door are five cells with rusty iron bars and little to no light. The only source was from the small opening at the top of each cell and the two flame lanterns that hung just next to the doorway. There are puddles between the cobblestone bricks, and it smells dank. There is a guard just off to the left rattling some keys as he unlocks one of the cells. My father and I approach him, a suddenly a squeezing feeling appears in my gut, clenching as my father begins to speak.

"Sebastian?"

"Yes, Papa?"

"What are we?"

"We are family?" I say in childish delight.

"No, separately, what are we?"

I think for a moment, trying to solve his riddle quickly, but also wondering what it had to do with where we were. Then I figure it out and say with glee, "We are vampires!"

"Very good my boy. Now can you tell me what that means?"

"I means... well it means," then I get flustered because I didn't know the answer to his question.

"It means our body cannot produce blood entirely on its own so we need to borrow." Then he pauses his expression stiffening, "It means we must drink of others to survive."

"Oh, is that why my fangs have come in Papa?"

"Exactly right son. I am going to teach you how to borrow from others."

Then he lets go of my hand and signals to the guard to open the cell door. He steps inside and returns pulling out a frail, filthy mortal boy. The boy has shackles on his wrists and his garments are worn and tattered. He looks miserable and frightened.

"We must drink of other to survive." He said again, this time in a stentorian tone. Then his eyes began to glow red, and his long sharp fangs emerged from his mouth, and he pierced the mortal boy's neck and began to drink. I screamed and began to cower away, turning to find there were two armed guards just behind me blocking my path.

"Drink!" My father yells, his lips now dripping with the life essence of another.

"No, Papa!" I scream in a shrill, deafening voice that echoed in the corridor. Pushing against the guards in an attempt to escape. Then I feel him grab me by the back of my neck and pull me rearward until I am face to face with the mortal boy. The boy looked more feeble than he had before.

"Drink!" my father shouts again.

"I can't!" I screech.

"You must!" He bellows.

"Papa! Please!" I say as I begin to cry, feeling the clench of my father's firm grip on the back of my neck.

He says nothing, he just grunts and shoves my tiny face into the nape of the boy's neck. I cringe and curl my lips in, feeling the dampness of the boy's blood smearing on my face. Not budging in my endeavor, my father throws me to the ground with a terrible grazing of the grimy stones.

"Then what good are you!" he said with a scowl. The feeling in my gut tightens until it reaches my soul, squeezing me until it is a knot deep within me. I get up from the floor and run out threw the threshold back up to the main hall, pushing past everyone in my wake. I run out to the stables and throw myself down in the hay. I cry and cry, so lost in my own emotions I momentarily lap up the substance dripping from my mouth. I taste the blood, and it fills me with a feeling of animalistic desire, and I love it.

I licked as much of the red liquor off my lips as I could salvage, feeling ravenous for more. When I heard the whiny of a nearby horse, and against all my efforts, I did the unspeakable; I drained the poor beast. Every last one of them.

"Sebastian!" My mother cries as she enters the scene to see me lying amongst the carcasses. Followed by my father wearing a maniacal and proud smirk. I stand, my eyes glowing red just as my fathers had, and drenched in the life force of prey. Feeling ashamed and guilty, but also knowing there was a part of me that enjoyed it. The violence and fear I had caused had me thirsty for more.

The knot inside clenched until I felt like I was going to choke. I ran into the woods, running as fast as my little feet could take me until I reached the river. I dropped to my knees and stared at my reflection in the water below. I could see the blood all over my face and the tears welling in my eyes. Then unable to hold back and cry out in pain, slamming both my fists into the water splashing uncontrollably. Cupping the water in my hands and rubbing my face aggressively as if to wash away my shame. I continued to sob knowing it was only a matter of time before I had to do the unspeakable again. Then once more I splashed uncontrollably in the river below.

Then the shimmer on the bathwater splashed as Jasper poured in another steaming pitch of water in the tub.

"There we are Little Bat. May I get you anything else my prince?" He says still holding the pitcher.

" I am a bit famished if you wouldn't mind fetching me something," I say, still feeling the knot yanking on my soul. Knowing my life would forever be a dance between the frenzy and my unwavering detest of my own existence.

Jasper hands me a goblet of blood and I look down into it seeing my reflection of shame and arbor looking up at me. So long as I must drink of others to survive, the memories of my life threaten to haunt me for eternity.

Chapter 1
Jezebel

I SIT IN THE FOYER WITH SEBASTIAN, WHO IS pouring me a cup of tea. I hear the clanging of the tea set and the creaking of the drink cart but am too numb to look. Perching on the sofa just across from the fireplace, a wooden coffee table is the only thing separating us from the opening in the wall in which the flames dance. I stare at the glow in a trace, listening to the mesmerizing crackling of the burning embers.

"Jezebel, are you okay?" Sebastian pipes up as he approaches me on the sofa, handing me a saucer with a steaming teacup of chamomile tea on it, taking the saucer I hold it on my lap. I can smell the sweet nectar of the honey and feel the steam on my face.

Breaking free of my flame-filled daze, I look down to see the translucent brown liquid and observe the shimmering caustics as they swirl in my cup. Then I look up at him with a new daze, as if searching for an answer to the question and expecting it to be written on his face. I am not even sure what question he asked, but still, I ponder for the answer. But all I see is his handsome features, wearing a look of helplessness and regret, brightened by the orange luminescence of the firelight. Not finding fulfillment, my gaze returns to the flames, still saying nothing I take a sip of my tea which is still perfectly hot.

"Jezebel," Sebastian drops to the spot on the couch next to me. "He won't be able to find us here, the house is under a cloaking spell. We are safe here. We are too strong when we are together, he does not stand a chance." Sebastian says in a compassionate hushed tone.

Unfazed, I sit silently still staring into the orange blaze, the flames seems to blur as my mind drifts back to the events earlier in the night on the rooftop.

"Thaddeus" Sebastian snarled.

"So nice to see you again old friend." The man with the yellow eyes growled back, smirking proudly.

"What are you doing here?" Sebastian responded, not seeming as delighted by his *old friends'* visit.

"You see that sweet fragile little thing behind you," he said gesturing to me. "I'll be taking her with me." Shocked and confused I look to Sebastian, hoping for a clue what this yellow-eyed man was talking about.

He says nothing, he just furrows his eyebrows in anger. Then looking at me Thaddeus says, "Come on love, don't you recognize me?"

"Why would I know you?" I say stepping out from behind Sebastian.

"Come on then give us a kiss!" He teased, puckering his lips, and smacking them at me as if I were a dog.

"What!" I exclaimed, disturbed by his invitation. Sebastian then pushed me back behind him, not once taking his eyes off Thaddeus.

"What do you want Thad?" Sebastian bellowed with disdain.

"I told you I came back for little Miss Briggita, or whatever her name is now. She is mine and you know it."

"She is not property!" Sebastian barks back, "Her name is Jezebel, and she is with me!"

"All right, easy now. Let's have a deal then. Let her decide, she'll choose me again you'll see." Then he let out a conniving chuckle and flashed the same proud smirk from before.

"How about let's not, and unfortunately for you, I have just reached my limit. I lost her before, I will not lose her again! Do you understand?" He paused briefly, "So, if you want her you are going to have to go through me." Sebastian challenged.

"My pleasure," Thaddeus responded delighted by the invitation for a fight.

Almost instantaneously he charged toward Sebastian, and Sebastian reciprocated the same ambition. Thaddeus offered the first blow as he cocked his fist back in the air and threw it into Sebastian's face. Sebastian ducked and dropped to his knees just in time, sliding under Thad's fist. His pants made a grating sound against the sand on the pavement of the rooftop.

Then returning to his feet as soon as he lost the momentum of the slide. Sebastian, not wasting any time, returned to the fight as he burrowed his fist deep into Thad's gut. Thaddeus bent against his will and gagged at the sickening feeling of being blasted in the stomach. Then after he recovered his breath, he grabbed Sebastian by the arm and leg, lifted him off the ground up over his shoulder, and threw him across the rooftop.

  I stood in anticipation watching as these two guys, these vampires, beat each other to a pulp. Punching, kicking, and throwing everything they got at each other. And for what, me; or Briggita is more likely the reason. I was still having a hard time accepting that I had one guy who enjoyed my conversation, as well as my company. Now this other guy drops out of the sky and is willing to fight for me. Yet all I could think about was how it wasn't me they were fighting over, it was Brigitta. *I need to know more about her, and I will, if I get out of this alive.*

  I wanted nothing more than to turn and run from the chaos, feeling scared and helpless, I was unsure what to do in the situation. Then in the midst of contemplating with my conscience, I remembered I am not as helpless as I feel. So, I corrected my stance, closed my eyes, took a deep breath through my nose, and conjured a fireball in both hands. Then

I heard a big thud that shook the building and cracked the cement on the rooftop just a hair. Startled by the sound I let out a small squeal, getting Sebastian's attention. Who was currently tying Thaddeus up in a headlock, tightening his grip as he peered across the rooftop to find something he didn't expect to see?

"Jezebel run!" He yelled in fear and panic. Even more confused by his outburst I turned to see what he was talking about. Just there a few yards from me is the ugliest creature I had ever seen.

At first, it is only a pair of blood red eyes, and fangs dripping in drool. It stalked closer towards me as its body materialized before my very eyes. The creature's body was furless, and its skin was pitch black and wrinkled. Having the appearance of dull black rubber. The only hair on the beast is the few tuffs that it has between its two narrow, pointy, erect ears. It walks on all fours and has long claws hanging off each of its toes, which scrap the ground as it moves; they are just as sharp as the fangs hanging from its furless snout. The creature's most noticeable feature however are the burning, blood-red eyes that bulge from its skull.

As it continued to get closer, I began to feel my heart start to pound in my chest. I stared at the beast, and suddenly I realized that this was the same monster from the parking garage. Only this time it is more than just eyes and teeth; it is the full ugly monstrosity.

"What is that thing?" I blurted out with fear, simultaneously wasting no time throwing the fiery ammunition I conjured at the monster. Missing the target both times. Conjuring more fireballs, I continuously blasted the creature as I heard Sebastian and Thaddeus grunting in the background. The monster didn't seem to be fazed by the fire at all and kept slowly stalking forward. I stepped backward as steadily as I could manage until I stumbled and collapsed to the ground. Trying to keep my fear at bay, I start scooting backward, trying not to lose eye contact with the beast.

"Gýmona!" Sebastian shouted, finally answering my question as he threw Thad off the side of the rooftop and rushed to my aid. He grabbed me by my arms and lifted me to my feet. Then with me in front of him, he ran full force toward the edge of the roof.

"Sebastian, what are you doing?" I exclaim in panic, not knowing what could be worse; being mauled by the creature or falling off the edge of the roof.

"Trust me!" He exclaimed as he took hold of my waist tightly and dived off the roof. Screaming my head off as we descend to the ground at an increasing rate. I covered my eyes with my hands, so I didn't have to see my face hit the pavement. Suddenly I felt a rush deep in my gut and a gentle breeze on my face. Uncovering my eyes just in time to see us suddenly lift upward toward the sky. Then as we leveled off and soared, I became aware that we were flying.

Berlin DiVittore

How are we flying above the city? I turn to Sebastian, who still had a firm hold on my waist, and I see a brilliant set of wings sprouting from his shoulder blades.

"You have wings? What!" I shriek astounded. Just when I started to think I was getting the hang of things and nothing new could happen, I was stunned.

Proven wrong by Sebastian's beautiful wings. They are twice his height from tip to tip, fully extended. Having the appearance of bats' wings, but with shiny black feathers across the front, which glistened with silver and iridescent hues in the moonlight.

We touched down in the courtyard of Sebastian's house, reuniting my body with gravity. Beginning our walk inside in silence, when suddenly my legs began to wobble, and I fell to the ground. Everything becomes a blur, and the world faded away. The last thing I saw before the world turned dark was Sebastian's handsome face. Then the flames in the fireplace blurred away and the memories became just that, memories.

"Jezebel, are you okay?" Sebastian's voice echoes in my ear, which brings my attention from the entrancing gaze of the shimmering flames back to him.

"Wha...what?" I say, blinking and shaking my head, pulling myself back to reality.

He just stares at me with a sliver of concern peering out through his eyes, anxiously waiting for me to answer his question. Sliding to the edge of the couch, I place my tea on the coffee table and push the blanket off my shoulders. Lastly, I brush my loose hair back out of my face and tuck it behind my ears. Taking a deep breath, I look him in the eye to let him know he has my full attention.

"Are you alright?" Sebastian repeats, but this time in a more heartfelt manner. "You have not said much since your fainting spell. I know this is all still new to you and I understand you need time to process."

Berlin DiVittore

Taking a deep breath, I gather my thoughts quickly and say, "Honestly, I'm a little shaken up by the events of the night. When I was getting ready for our date this was the last thing on my mind. I honestly wanted a break from all the supernatural mumbo-jumbo. I just wanted to go out and have a nice time with you away from the manor and magic stuff. But now that I think about it, I don't think I let myself fully comprehend the idea of being a *'witch'* and you being a *'vampire'*. I only convinced myself I had because I really like how you make me feel." Then I let out a sigh and continue, "I got so caught up in the *'fairytale'* of things that I didn't process *'the reality'*. I had wished my entire childhood that it could be possible, but just like a child, I forgot to consider how dangerous it could be. I was terrified on that roof tonight, and not just for myself but for you." I could feel the tears starting to pool in my eyes.

"Now on top of everything else, there is this creepy guy who thinks he's entitled to me. As if a person could be entitled to another somehow. He also thinks I'm what's-her-face behind the curtain in your cryptic magic room upstairs." I wipe my face as I start to feel fumed, I continue, "Then that demon from the parking garage was on the roof tonight and it wants to eat me! You got the crap kicked out of you and don't seem to be bothered by it. You're not even bruised or bleeding, which is abnormal in and of itself. To top it off you can freaking fly! Like what?" I say huffing out of breath finally running out of fumes. I stare at him and let out a big sigh.

"Okay, I think it's time for bed. Come on I'll walk you." He says standing and offering me his hand.

"No! Sebastian!" I blurt at him jumping to my feet, "For the first time since discovering my magic, I am truly beginning to understand who I am."

"You seem a little hysterical is all," Sebastian responds, stepping towards me to look me in the eye. "I know this is all happening very suddenly for you, seemingly even faster now that Thad is here. I think we need to rest and then in the morning, we can talk some more. I promise to answer all your questions." Then he grins at me and reaches his hand out as a way of reoffering to walk me to bed.

Admitting my defeat on the subject I let out another sigh and agree, "Fine."

Taking his hand and gazing into his golden eyes, somehow once again finding them calming amongst the chaos. We leave the foyer and make our way upstairs, walking in silence but still holding hands. Then Sebastian breaks the silent tension. "By the way, I did not get the *crap* kicked out of me." He retorts defending his honor. I giggle, smiling and shaking my head, feeling slightly better by his ability to make jokes and act so composed towards the events of the evening. I walk with him until we reach the door to my room, both of us remaining silent the entire distance.

Indulge: Book Two

"Here we are," he kisses my hand before letting it go. "Sleep well." Then turning to walk away, taking only a single step, before pivoting back to face me. "Jezebel, I'm sorry the night once again unfolded in an unforeseen manner. Not exactly what I envisioned for our first official date either. I promise to protect you with all that I have and more, just as I said before. Thaddeus won't come near you, I swear it."

Then he takes a brief pause as if to find the courage to say the next part. "However, on the off chance, it would bring me some comfort to know you are safe always. Would it be possible for you to consider sleeping here from this point forward? Just until we are rid of this new pest."

"If it brings you comfort, then yes I will," I respond pleasantly, almost in a teasing manner, before opening the door and slipping away into my room.

Closing the door slowly, peaking at him through the gap in the doorway until the door latches closed and all the light from the hall has been banished from my room. I turn to see the room cloaked in darkness. I begin to make my way toward the bed when suddenly there is a sound. There standing in the darkness at the end of the bed, is a figure. Still standing by the entrance I quickly flick on the lights, only to be slightly startled, then relieved it is only Eliza.

"Hello, Miss... I mean Jez. I am sorry I startled you, I was turning down the bed. Then I waited patiently for you to finish your conversation with Master Sebastian." Eliza states sweetly, smiling.

"No, that is alright. It has just been a long day, come to think of it, it has been a long month."

"I understand, I hope you rest well. Is there anything else I can do for you?"

"Just one thing, Eliza it would be very helpful if you could please work with the lights on. I startle easily as you now know." I say as politely as I can, trying not to make it sound as harsh as it felt.

"Oh, yes of course. I don't need the light, so I often overlook the importance of them, but in consideration for your human eyes, I will remember next time."

"Thank you," I say, feeling a little awkward about the conversation.

"Will there be anything else?"

"No, I think that will be all. Thank you."

"Very well, should you need anything just ring for me and I shall be here to assist you. Goodnight miss." Eliza says before exiting the room.

"Goodnight." I politely say under my breath knowing she has already left the room.

Then I dress into some plum purple sleep shorts and a matching tank top and crawl into bed. I lay there looking up seeing only the top of the canopy bed frame. My eyes slowly close as I begin to drift away. When suddenly I am alarmed once more by a rustling noise. I sit up to look around and see nothing but an empty dark room. Trying to focus on my sleep to avoid paranoia but only making matters worse.

Then I have an idea, I try to conjure a blue glowing ball, like the one that helped me find Sebastian in the mirror maze. However, I am unsure of how I conjured it, so I come up with nothing. So, I ring the bell for Eliza, and she arrives at my room almost immediately.

"What can I do for you miss?" She asks pleasantly.

"Sorry to bug you again, but could you show me the way to Sebastian's room please?"

"It is no bother. It is right this way." Saying as she points and heads down the hall to the left. We only walk a few doors down before she stops. "Here you go Miss... I mean Jez." Pausing to let out a small giggle, "That is hard to get used to doing."

"That's alright if it's too difficult 'Miss' is fine too."

"Okay, Miss. Well, here we are at the Master Sebastian's room." Leaning in a little she whispers, "You might want to knock first; he doesn't like to be bothered when he is in his chambers."

"Oh, thanks for the tip." Then she curtsies and makes her way back down the hall fading into the dim lights. I turn, standing in front of the closed double doors, I take a deep breath and lightly tap on the door.

Chapter 2
Sebastian

I PACE BACK AND FORTH IN FRONT OF THE fire of my chambers, thinking about everything that Jezebel had just said to me. Gripping tightly to the amulet that I had meant to give to Jezebel before our date. Thinking back to our past dates and not understanding how everything always seemed to go so awry when we were together. Yet that did not stop my heart from falling for her once more.

How easy it was for my heart to bring back the feelings we once shared in another life; but I doubt she feels the same. *How do I tell her the truth? Or should I continue to hide my feelings from her?* I suppose for her it is quite different for she is only just meeting me, while I have known her likeness for centuries.

Then I take a deep breath, now is not the time, I think to myself. She is in danger because I could not allow myself to stay away. I knew I should have just accepted the knowledge that she was in that Chinese restaurant and let her move on without interfering, letting her forget about me. A mistake I am all too familiar with but that kiss we shared at the concert was so electric. I could not let my heart forget and let go of her again. *Could I allow myself to be that selfish? Could I allow myself to keep her in harm's way, just to be near her? Even more than that, could I let the cycle end? Or is it bigger than both of us?*

"No, I cannot keep letting this happen to her," I whispered aloud to myself. "She needs to increase her power but the only way she can do that is a Blood Ritual. She is not yet strong enough or experienced enough for that type of magic, it could kill her." Then amid my pacing, I am interrupted by a small tapping on the door.

Confused, I quickly hide the amulet in a wooden box on the mantel above the fireplace and rush to the door. Opening the door to find Jezebel standing shyly outside in her pajamas.

"Jezebel?" I ask confused, "I thought you went to bed?"

"May I come in?" She inquires softly but still persistently.

"Of course," I say stepping aside allowing her to enter the foyer of my room. She looks around like she always does when discovering a new room. Then she sits slightly off the edge of the sofa just across from the fireplace.

"Is something the matter?" I ask, worried by her silence.

"I can't sleep, and I don't want to be alone right now." Saying coyly, assumingly not expressing to me the whole truth. However, in order not to offend her, I brush it off and move on.

"I acknowledge the challenges you have experienced, going through so much within such a brief period of time. I am however pleased to know you feel safe enough to confide in me for comfort."

"I do Sebastian. You know it is the strangest thing, from the moment we met I instantly felt safe with you, like I could say anything to you, and you would totally get me."

"Well, seeing as neither of us will be getting much rest tonight. May I suggest calling down to Jasper and requesting he bring up some 'comfort food'? What would you li…" she then cuts me off before I can finish my question.

"Oh, Sebastian! That is so sweet, but I just couldn't. I'm imposing enough as it is."

"You are anything but an imposition. Please, I insist. What will it be?"

Blushing with a nervous shrug she says, "I would really love some chocolate chip cookies with some milk, please."

"Alright, then cookies you shall have." I ring the call bell to the kitchen, and not a moment later Jasper appears at my door. I pass along Miss Jones' request, and he returns with a tray just as promptly as he had appeared before. I take the tray with Jezebel's treat, along with some freshly squeezed steak in a glass goblet for me.

Setting the tray down on the coffee table just in front of us. Joining Jezebel on the sofa, we sit facing one another. Enjoying our spoils and each other's company. We chat freely, avoiding the world and all its future troubles. We are just about finished with the last of our treats when Jezebel lets out a big yawn.

"Are you relaxed enough that you think you might be able to get some sleep?"

"Yes, I think I am. Thanks, Sebastian for comforting me and helping me through my insomnia."

"It was my pleasure," I say sincerely pleased by her gratitude.

"I don't really have that many people who I can really lean on, well except Ashton of course. Even still I have only known her for seven years, which isn't really that long. So, anyway I just..." She begins to ramble on about her feelings of graciousness, but I cannot help but become distracted by her plump juicy lips. Then I get lost in her big pale green eyes. Oh, and how I am suddenly yearning to caress her skin with my lips.

"You know what I mean Sebastian?" I nod in agreement, even though I have lost track of what she is saying.

Berlin DiVittore

She continues talking and I see her mouth moving but I do not hear any of the words she is saying because I have become too entranced with her skin. I trace her lips with my eyes, and then my eyes seem to find their way to her neck. I am mesmerized as the glow from the fireplace illuminates her skin, highlighting its soft contours.

My blood is beginning to rush, and my body feels warm, but my eyes cannot stop themselves. They drift even further from her neck down to her silky-smooth shoulders. My eyes become greedy as they fall to her chest. Observing them closely I take in every detail, watching as her body shift as she speaks. It was not until just now that I realized her breasts.

In all the time we have spent together, I have yet to notice them. They are not that large, but who honestly cares about that anyway? They are perky and blanketed by the same caramel, silky-smooth skin that covers her whole body. *Oh, and what a curvy beautiful body it is*, I think to myself.

"Are you even listening to me?" she says interrupting my kinky inner monologue, just in time too.

"Sorry, what?" is all I think to say, quickly lifting my eyes to her face.

"I guess that means no," she says seeming amused but disappointed. Having no response, I fall back to my previous train of thought and am once again distracted by her chest.

"Sebastian!" she wails in a cheeky tone, sliding closer to me on the sofa and waving her hand in front of my eyes, drawing my attention once more back up to her face. She smiles and bites her bottom lip. *Oh, come on that is just not fair*, I think to myself.

"Do you see something you like?" she teases, batting her eyes and giving her chest a slight shimmy.

"Uh, no I was listening. You were talking about friends and …" I stop and sigh, smirking at her trying my best to hold my ground. Then having finally caught up, I realize have been caught; I fold. "Actually yes, I was just observing your striking features. It has been a while since my eyes have been able to gaze upon your beautiful face."

"Oh, my beautiful face? Amongst other things I presume?" She says, once again giving her chest a quick shimmy in my direction.

"Yes, you have very nice tits…ah traits." I quickly correct my words. Hoping she did not catch my blunder, but as she lets out a little snicker, it is abundantly clear that she did. Even still I try to maintain my composure and pretend that the incident did not occur and carry on as usual. "I appreciate the opportunity to engage in meaningful discussion. It has been a pleasure to spend this time with you."

"I have really enjoyed this time with you as well." She says sliding closer, evidently aware of my true mindset, unwilling to let go of the matter at hand.

"Jezebel, don't you think you better... go to bed...now," I say trying not to give in to my desires but my words trickling off as I am once more preoccupied by her starry gaze and voluptuous lips.

Before I can stop myself, I find myself all at once cupping her face with my hands and eagerly bringing my lips to hers. Thrilled to finally get the chance to taste her lips again. We share in a sweet, delectable kiss. Her soft lips begin to entangle themselves and dance with mine.

She gently places her hands on my chest, obviously a little surprised by the sensual collision of our mouths. Only to find seconds later she is leaning into me, deepening our embrace. Both of us quickly becoming mesmerized with the other, my hands begin to drift, finding her lower back and pulling her toward me.

Then to my surprise, she climbs on my lap, straddling me with her legs. Grabbing at the nape of my neck, running her hands up the back of my head, and combing her fingers through my hair, moaning at the deep carnal pleasure. I take this as my cue to fill my hands with her exceptional ass. Our lips still entangled with each other, and my lips proceed to work their way down her body to her chest. Which I still have not been able to get out of my head.

Along the way, I find the collar of her neck, and against all my instincts I open my mouth to take a taste.

"Ouch!" She exclaims, jumping off my lap and pressing her hand against her neck, "Did you bite me?"

Feeling both embarrassed and enraged I look away feeling ashamed. Saying nothing at first, but then when confronted with my own humiliation all I can manage to say is, "I suppose I did, didn't I?"

"Maybe we did get a little carried away." She says in my defense. Then wiping her neck with her hand and looking at it; undoubtedly checking for blood.

"Do not do that!" I roar as I get up from the sofa and make my way to the closed curtains that separate the bed chamber from the foyer of my room. My feet stomping the wooden slates of the floor, reverberating the room with a resounding and echoing thump.

"Do what?" she asks bewildered.

I say nothing, just continue to retreat behind the curtains. Throwing them back and forcing my way through the doorway.

"Sebastian! Sebastian!" She shouts my name, chasing me and trying to probe a response out of me. I ignore her, not interested in pursuing this conversation any further; but she persists. "Sebastian!" Unable to handle her sweet voice nagging me any longer I turn and snap.

"Don't be my savior! I do not need you to pretend like it is acceptable that I am a monster! I am a repulsive, horrible, beast and there is no point in pretending I am not!" I huff out of breath; I stand frozen next to my bed staring at her sweet face, trying to gauge her expression in the darkness of the room.

She stands before me, momentarily perplexed. Then, her demeanor softens as she reaches for me and says, "That is not how I feel about you."

"Well, you should, because it is the truth," I say in disbelief of her statement. Pulling away from her reach, I began to pace, still feeling the fumes of rage boiling in my body.

"No!" She exclaims, tenaciously. "You are beautiful and kind. You have done nothing but try to protect me since we met."

"I am also the reason you've been in danger since we met!" I counter.

"No, you are wrong, and I love you." With those words she spoke aloud we both halted immediately and looked at each other stunned. She stood blushing, both her hands immediately covering her mouth as if to prevent any more accidental confessions.

I approach her, placing my hands gently on her petite shoulders, she gazes up at me still blushing removing her hands from her mouth and begins biting her bottom lip.

"You what?"

"I...I love you." She declares yet again with a nervous smile. Hearing her say it a second time, still a little unsure, a feeling washes over me like a cleansing ritual. Melting away all the current feelings of doubt and dismay and leaving just one in its place. Love.

"I love you too." Then we delicately embrace in a loving kiss, holding each other so gracefully. Unlike the passionate encounter we shared in front of the fire just moments ago, this embrace was soft, sweet, and loving. Pulling away to look into each other's eyes, not with the usual fondness but in a way that feels warmer and more electric.

Berlin DiVittore

She smiles at me and strokes my face with her warm hand. The delicate feeling of her soft warmth against my skin makes me feel the most human I have ever felt.

She speaks softly, "You are not a monster, any more than I am. *I* am not in danger because of *you*. *We* are in danger *together*. I may be new and inexperienced, but I know that this is a battle I want to fight because, for the first time in my life, I have something worth fighting for. For the first time I am doing *exactly* what I know I was always meant to do." Then once more she smiles at me, looking into my soul and I begin to feel something that in all my years I have never experienced.

Taking both her hands in mine, I escort her to my bed. I then lay down and opened my arms to her, not only to let her decide but also to let her know I wanted to hold her. As she climbs onto the bed, I lovingly enfold her in my arms, and we drift off to sleep in a comforting embrace, finding solace in each other's presence.

Chapter 3
Jezebel

O PENING MY EYES, UNFAMILIAR WITH MY surroundings. Blinking forcefully a few times to wash away the sleepiness in my eyes. Then regaining full awareness, I suddenly remember I am in Sebastian's bed. His arms are still wrapped around me, as I lay on his bicep like a pillow while he is still fast asleep. One of my hands is tucked close to my chest, the other draped on my abdomen, our legs intertwined like Twizzlers.

I nuzzle up against his chest with my cheek, remembering last night and how sweet he was to let me spend some time here with him; and all the events that followed. Every savory kiss we shared, all the heartfelt talks and laughs, and his voice saying he loved me. Even the short tryst on the couch, him biting my neck and how secretly thrilling it was for me. Then just as I was getting cozy, I hear a small noise across the room by the closet, just beyond the end of the bed. So, without disturbing Sebastian's slumber I leave the bed and peak over the baseboard.

Rolling around on the ground just in front of the closet doors is a beautiful black cat, stretching out. I approach him calmly, trying not to startle the little guy but to my surprise, he approaches me without hesitation. Still curious and eager to pet him, I pick him up and cradle him in my arms.

"Wow aren't you just the sweetest little kitty," I whispered gently as I ran my hand over the cat's fur, feeling the softness and hearing the soothing sound of its purring.

"I knew you two would find each other eventually," Sebastian says sitting on the bed observing.

Pleasantly surprised I turn around, and grin at him in amusement, "What are you talking about?" I inquire.

"Witches have Familiars, and this little guy is yours."

"What is a *Familiar* exactly?"

"A *Familiar Spirit* is a supernatural entity, usually in the form of an animal, that is meant to aid and protect a witch on their journey."

"Oh. Well, how did you know he was mine?"

"Well, because he was also Brig...."

"Brigitta's," I interrupt him with a touch too much disdain. Then realizing I had already exposed more than I wanted to, I gently put the cat down and begin to make my exit from the room. Unsuccessful in my getaway when suddenly my escape route is blocked by Sebastian. He is standing in the doorway with his arms crossed, giving me a smug look.

"What?" I asked, innocently trying my best to hide my feelings but realizing that it wasn't going to be that easy.

Changing tactics I huff, cock my head, put my hands on my hips, and poutingly I say, "I forgot how fast you are."

He remains silent, responding only with a cocky grin and boastful chuckle. I came to the realization that this was not going to be a simple task. Frustrated, I let out a heavy sigh, crossed my arms, pivoted around, and wearily dropped down onto the bench at the foot of his bed. "Fine," I begin, then inhale deeply, "I've clearly ratted myself out, so no point trying to hide it anymore. I kind of hate Brigitta."

"What?" He states confused with a slight laugh, "How can you hate an individual that first of all you have never encountered? But particularly when that individual is an inherently a part of you?"

"That is exactly why I do. Everything before I met you was *only* mine, but everything after somehow always ends up being some *'hand-me-down'* thing. I don't even know if what I feel or think anymore is original because I am just this replicated instrument of the universe. It's not fair."

Indulge: Book Two

"I see," He responds plainly. Then he advances into the room and then finally sits down beside me.

"Sebastian, I have been reluctant to admit this only because I am not sure if when you look at me you see *me*, or if you see *her*. It's hard enough dealing with someone's exe, now I realize it's even harder when she looks just like you."

He takes a deep breath, holds both my hands in his, and says, "I am going to be candid and express my current perspective with you. At first, it was hard to see anyone other than her. However, upon understanding your unique qualities Jezebel, and how different you are. I now only see you. Last night when I said, 'I love you', I was directing that statement towards you; and you alone. It was a sentiment that far eclipsed any previous expressions directed towards Brigitta."

"Really?" I say blushing, trying to fight the tickling of the butterflies he was making me feel.

"I promise." He says sweetly, grinning at me.

"I am so relieved to hear you say that." Feeling better about the situation with those few words, I felt able to continue with my day. "You always know exactly what to say and even more, what I need to hear."

"Well, it's just a matter of honesty, and I will give that always."

"Thank you." Then we share sweet glances, and I feel the cat begin to rub against my leg. I peer down at him, and scratch between his ears, and I can hear the gentle rumble as he begins to purr. "Anyway, I have to go get ready. I will see you later." I turn my attention back to Sebastian, kiss him on the cheek, and make my way out the door.

Walking the short distance down the hall, I enter my bedroom and quickly get ready for the day. Then I speed toward the entrance of the manor. I rush toward the front door, but my progress is delayed once again by Sebastian, who is standing in my path.

"Hello again, you look ravishing today," he says with a sideway flirtatious smirk, ignoring my annoyed reaction to his interference.

"Thanks." I say still a touch annoyed, "Um, I don't have time for breakfast, so I am just gonna head out." Then I try to stalk around him, but he counteracts.

"I have some of my own business that requires my attention today as well. Will I still see you this evening?"

"Yes, I will see you later," I say, reaching around him for the doorknob, but he blocks me again. "What?" I squeal, getting a little more peeved. The feeling quickly dissipates as it is replaced by amusement. I look at him as he stands with his eyes closed softly and his lips puckering, waiting for a kiss. I give him a firm peck before he smiles at me and disappears into his office just to the left of the front door. I watch him adoringly, before remembering I was in a rush.

Then just as I reach out for the door handle, Jasper suddenly calls out my name.

"Miss Jones." Startled by his deep booming voice. I jump centimeters out of my skin before collecting myself with a relieving breath and turning to face him.

"Yes, Jasper?" I say confused but curious.

"Please be safe out there and return posthaste." He speaks sternly but with compassion.

"Yes, of course. I'm sure I will be fine; I doubt *what's-his-face* is brave enough to attack me during the day and in public. Besides, I'm just going straight home. Then I'll be with Ashton the rest of the day." I say reassuringly in the most convincing voice I can muster.

"You don't know him like I do, and his name is Thaddeus," Sebastian calls out, emerging from the doorway of his study.

"You're so sweet for caring so much for my safety, both of you. Also, I think I'm gonna stick with '*what's-his-face*'."

"I do indeed have a genuine concern for your well-being, and ensuring your security is of utmost importance to me. So, I wish you to have this and never take it off." He says, holding out a necklace with a beautiful tear-shaped sapphire, encased in a beautiful silver setting. He places it in the palm of my hand, so I can admire it closer. He continues, "It is a protection amulet made from the same jewel as the crescent amulet of your ancestors. It is charged by moonlight and will protect you at all the times I cannot."

"And recharge all the times you can!" I exclaim, finishing his sentence for him with a delighted smile. "Thank you it's beautiful, but isn't it kind of big?" I say looking at the blue gemstone in my palm the size of a half-dollar.

"Of course. You try containing the potent energy of the moon within a diminutive, feeble stone?"

"I might just take you up on that challenge." He responds with a chuckle and an intrigued expression.

"You want to know the best part?" he prompts, as he takes it and places the necklace around my neck.

"Sure, what is the best part?"

"You, sweet Jezebel, are the first to wear it." He says after clasping it and gazing at me lovingly. Feeling so heard; it takes all the strength I have not to burst into tears at his romantic gesture.

"Thank you," I say again this time with more compassion. "I will wear it proudly and never take it off."

"You are most welcome. Now I do have some paperwork I have to get to, and you need to head out for work." He kisses my cheek softly, and I make my final exit. I climb into the backseat of his car and Jasper drives me straight home. All the way I think of the butterflies I feel for Sebastian. Suddenly I realize Ashton is probably really pissed and thinks I ditched our double date, because I kind of did.

I walk in the front door to see Ashton making out with her date on the living room floor, in her full birthday suit.

"Oh, my goddess!" I shout, quickly shielding my eyes with my hand. "Ash! Really on the living room floor, I walk around here! Barefoot!"

"Hey!" She says turning to acknowledge my sudden presence, "Sorry. Oh, how were things with Sebastian? I'm guessing you guys took off… for well, some naked alone time." She says casually, clearly unfazed by my disruption of her private event. Then peaking between my fingers, I see her making goo-goo eyes at Damien, who was also buck naked.

"Gross! No!" I say clamping my fingers shut, wondering why I haven't learned after all these years with her. Turning away still averting my eyes, I blindly start making my way to my bedroom.

"Oh, come on! You gonna tell me nothing happened between you too?" She prompts nonchalantly as if I had *not* just caught her tongue wrestling a stranger with her bare biscuits hanging out.

"No, something happened but I'm not gonna talk about it with you, now, like this," I call out to her, just before finally slipping away behind the naked free zone of my closed bedroom door. I take a deep breath and cringe, shaking off yet another pornography mental image of my roomie and her many playmates.

I waste no time getting reacquainted with the familiar surroundings of my bedroom. I mean Sebastian's is nice, but it is almost too nice, sometimes it feels like I'm staying in a hotel. However, sleeping in his bed last night was so wonderful. He always smells so good, and for being a vampire he can be surprisingly warm. I feel so comfortable when he is near, it is almost too good to be true.

This led me to briefly ponder whether that is because we are magically programmed that way or because I have a genuine love for him. Something he has yet to confirm, even during my recent rant. The thought sat with me, maybe I do love him because I'm *supposed* to love him not because *I do*. Maybe a small part of me still thought that his attraction toward me was because I reminded him of Brigitta.

I began stoking the amulet that Sebastian had just gifted me, remembering his loving gesture. Mystified by the thoughts banging around in my head I push them aside and stop thinking about them before I ruin everything, again. I pack a quick overnight bag since I am going to stay at Sebastian's for a while.

Then grabbing my script, I head out to the living room, but not before making sure the coast is clear of all unclothed persons. I crack my door open and call out into the living space to anyone who might be present.

"Ashton! Is everyone decent? And by decent, I mean wearing clothes?" I don't hear a reply, so I assume that she has taken her playmate elsewhere. I step out of my room slowly, taking extra precautions. Sure enough, the room is empty. After I make the room suitable again, I plant myself down on the couch and get comfy with my script.

"I can't believe you're actually sitting there after everything you just saw?" Ashton jokes as she enters the room in her robe.

"I brought a friend," I say holding up a spray can of disinfectant, not having taken my eyes off my script. "Trust me, I'm an expert at this point. I hosed the area down thoroughly." I say, finally pulling my eyes from the tiny paper book and placing the can back down next to me.

"Sorry, you had to see that." She says simply, as she takes a seat on the coffee table in front of me.

"Are you? Are you really?" I sass her as I place my study materials to the side.

"No. No, I am not." Then we stare at each other before we both burst into a quick giggle. "Look, if I had known you were coming home, I would have made sure we took the party elsewhere, but spur of the moment is spur of the moment."

"I know exactly what you mean," I say reminiscing the memory of last night's tryst.

"Do I get to know some of the dirty little details of *your* night?"

"It was nothing just a kiss or two." She looks at me in disbelief, a look that just says she knows I am downplaying it. "It was just a kiss, an extremely steamy, passionate kiss. There might have also been some groping and biting," I say teasingly, intentionally being very vague.

"That's what I'm talking about! Tell me more?" she squeals, urging for additional information. But being the kind who doesn't usually *'kiss and tell'* I roll my eyes at her instead. Then she makes a puppy dog face clasping her hands together desperately begging me for more.

"Yes, we shared a kiss, but the best part of the night were the cuddles, and we said *the words*."

"Words? What words?" She says, seeming disappointed by my refusal to share more while also appearing confused.

"Yes. There are three of them and one of them starts with an 'L'."

"Ah, you mean *those* words." Taking a moment to process and catch up, then says, "Hey, wait, you said you love him already? You only just met him!"

"It's not the same thing, we were *made* for each other."

"Oh hun, I know everyone feels that way at first." She replies as if trying to let me down easily.

"No, I mean we were *literally* made for each other," I explain slowly, as she looks at me with genuine shock still looking a little confused.

"What do you mean, *literally*?"

Then speaking quickly, I explain a summarized version of what Sebastian recently told me, "Okay, so a long time ago, like an exceptionally long time ago, there were these two clans. One Vamps and the other Witches, and they shared abilities in order to save this dying chick's life. But to do that she had to share her soul with the Vampire prince. Like they *literally* ripped his soul in half like it was a sandwich or something, and then filled in the new halves with one weaved from stars. Sebastian and I are the recycled copies of those two souls." I huff out of breath.

Ashton says nothing, she just stares with a stunned look on her face. I wait for her eye to start twitching, but it doesn't. Then she stands and begins to pace around the coffee table. After taking a couple of laps, she sits back down and blurts, "You literally have a guy that was *made* for you, and I'm over here recycling boyfriends and getting caught naked in the living room?"

"How did this suddenly get turned back to you," I say selfishly, feeling offended but her comment.

"Oh, yes because everything is about *Jezebel* all the time I forgot. It's not like you have everything! You have magical powers for shit's sake, if that's not enough you have a guy who was *literally* made for you. Sorry if I am feeling a little jilted." She says jumping back to her feet in a heated fashion.

"Just a couple weeks ago I broke up with the guy I thought I was going to marry, lost a job that I worked ridiculously hard for, and found out I'm a witch."

"You're really complaining about breaking up with your sex-crazed-exe when you're with a guy that looks like Sebastian. Your bed is not even cold yet and you're already saying 'I love you' to him. Also, how dare I take pity on you and give you a freaking job, and something you'd actually enjoy might I add. Now I don't have to hear you complain about *Crazy-Office-Barbie* every day. Oh, and you're a witch, how horrible. When do you get the warts on your face?"

"Probably after you stop whoring it about in the living room!" I retort matching her energy as I stand up. Ashton, clearly feeling wounded, says nothing, only gasps and glares.

So, I continue, "I am a witch, and it's not all fun and games. It's actually quite hard and dangerous, I could die. And as hot as Sebastian is, he is a freaking vampire and that is a little intimidating compared to Michael. He literally bit me last night, not in the kinky way, in the you're my dinner kind of way. Michael never wanted to eat me! Thank you very much for the job by the way. I do enjoy it!" I shout furiously causing the light bulbs in the lighting fixture on the ceiling to burst and the room to go dim.

We both let out a scream, as sparks fell to the ground before slowly dissipating. Shortly after the lamp across the room flicked on to reveal Ashton and I huddled together on the couch.

"What the hell was that?" Damien said, now fully clothed. His hand still resting on the lamp, pausing briefly as his suspicious gaze sweeps over us, before making his way cautiously in our direction. Ashton and I look each other in the eye, still shaken and dumbfounded for words. Breaking our hold on each other and finding our wits, we stand. Then to justify the situation and not cause a fuss I say, "Oh, that was nothing, probably just bought the wrong bulbs or something."

"You know us girls can't be trusted to do anything not in the kitchen," Ashton adds nervously. Then I glare at her completely sexist statement. "What?" I mouth to her, and she glares back at me realizing how ridiculous she sounds. So, I chime in trying to recover from her statement.

"Anyway! It's almost 10:30 and we need to head out to work, it was nice of you to visit us."

"Yes, thanks for the date and the sex. I'll call you." She says pushing him out the door.

"Thanks for the sex? Not in the kitchen? Well, we shouldn't expect a call for you to advocate the feminist movement anytime soon." I taunt sarcastically, still a little steamed from our argument.

"I was stumped okay. What am I supposed to say, my roommate's a witch and blew them up with her witchy voodoo?"

"No, but you are also not supposed to say things that take us back to the 1950's. Go get dressed we're gonna be late." Not having a comeback, she just sticks her tongue at me and stomps off to her room like a five-year-old girl.

We arrive at the theatre just in time for rehearsal. Ashton addresses everyone; some groan at her tardiness, while others greet her eagerly. We all prepare for dress rehearsal by changing into our costumes. We jump from scene to scene as fast as we can, an exercise to try our best at being off book. I find this exercise to be particularly difficult as I have only just been cast and am not quite yet there.

After a long day of doing two run-throughs in full costume. We all start to feel like a broken record. Sensing the energy in the room, Ashton calls it a day, and we all gather at the front of the stage for Ashton's daily announcements and closing statements.

As I am still adjusting to the new dynamic of having my best friend and roommate also be my boss, I find myself trying to navigate through this unique situation. Despite the initial challenges, I am beginning to build strong connections with the other cast members, which is helping me adapt and integrate into my role more seamlessly.

"Great job everyone! It looks great, just remember to annunciate, I'm talking to you Jerry," Ashton says shamelessly pointing to a member of the cast, "as well as making sure you are drinking plenty of water. We don't want any hoarse voices on opening night. Speaking of which, we open this weekend, and every weekend for the next month. Now the first show is always the hardest, but it is also the most exciting, especially for those of you who have not performed on stage before. If you wish to reserve any tickets take it up with Whitney, our stage manager. There will be an after-party in the lobby which your guests may also attend. Any questions?" The theatre grew quiet, "Okay, great! Goodnight, everyone. Now go change you look like a bunch of freaks."

  The huddle disperses with a giggle at Ashton's sassy retort. I jump off the stage and approach Ashton who is talking to her stage manager. After waiting for them to finish she looks at me, "Yes?"

  "I just want to apologize for our fight this morning, it is an adjustment, my new identity."

"I know, I'm sorry too. I will admit I am pretty jealous of your new guy and everything, not to mention the…" Then taking a brief pause to look to see if anyone is in earshot she finishes, "Voodoo."

"Thanks. I am happy. We will also need to work out a code word or something so you can stop saying 'voodoo'. Friends?" I say, opening my arms and inviting her to a hug.

"Friends? We are sisters!" Then she embraces me, being forced back by the thousands of layers of tulle around my waist.

"Whoa, I didn't realize you were packing south of the border there."

"Ashton!" I blurted, caught off guard but not surprised by her subtle innuendo.

"What? I mean it's like down boy." She states touching the stiffness of my tutu, "Ruff, ruff, ruff!" Then I notice people starting to stare as she proceeds barking and humping my costume. Feeling the tension of the awkward glances I shout, "Okay, that's enough! Get off!" I say, pushing her away and heading for my dressing room. Feeling comforted by the knowledge that her filthy remark and gesture indicated our relationship was back on track.

After changing and reserving a ticket for Sebastian, Ash and I head home. As we are parking I get a text message.

'Come to the roof of your building. -SB'

'On my way." I text back.

Feeling both delighted and interested by the invitation. I can feel the fluttering around in my stomach just at the thought of seeing Sebastian again. Not only that but he clearly could not wait to see me. This made the butterflies dance with such a fury I thought I would burst.

Chapter 4
Jezebel

THE STAIRS TO THE ROOF ARE ON THE TOP floor so I part ways with Ashton in the elevator and make my way up. Opening the door, I see Sebastian standing on the edge of the building staring out at the city lights as the last beam of sunlight dips beneath the horizon.

I observe him standing on the edge, poised and relaxed. His hands casually tucked into the pockets of his pants, while a gentle bay breeze tousles his dark, wavy hair. The moonlight gleaming across his features, accentuating his chiseled jawline, and casting shadows beneath his brooding eyes. It was a moment frozen in time, as he gazed musingly at the horizon, lost in the beauty of the world before him.

"Hey. What's up?" I ask casually, as I approach him from behind.

"Come up here with me." He states, reaching his hand out for mine.

"Uh-uh, no way," I respond skittishly, stepping back and hiding my hands behind my back. Feeling the knot in my stomach from our last jump off the roof not that long ago.

"Come on you'll be fine."

I clench my fist and bite my bottom lip, trying hard not to look him in the eye and fall prey to his convincing gaze, but all at once, I lose the upper hand with my conscience, looking at him. His amber eyes twinkle and his sideway grin lures me in, "Okay, fine." Taking his still outreached hand, I climb up on the ledge and look at the long way down. My heart begins to race, and my grip on his hand tightens.

"That is not what I wanted to show you, this is." He lifts my head by placing the back of two fingers under my chin. My eyes lifting from the dark street below, up to the glittering stars that seem to blend with the oranges and yellows of the city lights.

"See you can see them here too." He says softly as he begins to kiss my neck as I continue peering up into the sky.

"Stop it, we are gonna fall. We can't all fly like you can."

"Don't be so sure of that." He says as he pulls the sapphire amulet out of my cleavage, exposing it to the moonlight.

"Wait, now *I* can fly? How?"

"How can you move chairs with your mind? Or hold fire in the palm of your hand?"

"Teach me?" I persist playfully.

"Close your eyes and remember your trigger. Envision being untethered from earth's gripping hold on your body. Focusing on that vision slowly lift onto your toes, spread your arms, take a deep breath, and stay calm." Then there is a moment of silence, as I feel him guiding my arms out. Next, I hear the sound of his wings unfolding and smile at the thrilling buzz of adrenaline.

"Do you trust me?" he whispers directly into my ear, his warm breath sending shivers down my spine. Then feeling at ease as he places his strong hands delicately on my lower back. I give a slight nod enchanted by the flutter of romance once again present in my stomach, then refocusing on my trigger. Suddenly he gives me a quick nudge off the roof edge. Startled by my unexpected free fall off the ledge.

I open my eyes to see myself hovering in midair just a couple of stories from the roof. I look up to see him squatting on the edge looking down at me, his brilliant wings extended, and an amused grin plastered on his face, evidently pleased by his little trick.

I give a push upward, feeling the chilling breeze on my face, as I thrust a little higher than I had aimed. Sebastian catching me with his strong grip on my arm. Then holding onto me like a balloon he pulls me in his direction, my lips meeting his before my feet even have time to fall under me. Our embrace aligns as my feet find their way back to his. Our toes click together as I stand on hit boots still slightly hovering in mid-air.

I take his hands in mine, our lips still locked. I push backward, forcing him to follow me away from the rooftop ledge, our hands tightly fused but the kiss breaking off. I let out a sweet laugh having gotten my revenge.

"That was not very nice." He responds while gliding through the air with me after first catching his breath and flapping his magnificent wings.

"You pushed me first!" I tease letting go of his hand and shooting up into the clouds. Feeling the icy gusts of air brushing my cheeks, and warm tears escaping the corners of my eyes at the sudden rush of wind."

"We will have to get you some goggles or something." He says with a chuckle as he wipes the tears away with his thumbs. "Now, where were we?" He taunts as he leans his face in, to finish our embrace. His hands finding their way down around my bum, forcing me into him. His large hands attempting to cup each cheek in its entirety, making me moan with delight.

Separating our lips but still holding tightly onto one another, we gaze into each other's eyes. His hands sliding up to my lower back, he holds me lovingly. We hover amongst the diamonds in the sky before I hear him speak.

"See, you can fly." He says teasing me, while his wings flap creating a slight breeze.

"Only because you're such a good teacher." I say wittingly with a grin, "By far my favorite lesson." He says nothing, just smiles affectionately.

"How was work?" He then asks casually. I smile with a giggle. "What is so funny?" He queries.

"I never thought that I would ever have this conversation while hovering hundreds of miles in the air above the city."

"It is a bit different." He teases with a chuckle, releasing my waist.

"Can we just enjoy the moment and talk about it later?" I say redirecting his attention.

"Of course." He states understandingly.

Then after a brief silence, I tap my hand on his shoulder "You're it!" I shout before swiftly flying away.

"That's not fair," he shouts speeding after me.

Indulge: Book Two

He chases me through the clouds and then down around the tall buildings of the city. We finally touch down in the courtyard behind his mansion, amongst the trimmed hedges that make up the brilliant labyrinth. Trying to catch my breath, my head suddenly starts to feel fuzzy, and my legs begin to wobble. I try to walk it off, but I fall toward the ground, luckily Sebastian catches me.

"Okay, you need a moment's rest." He states lifting me into a cradle and carrying me to the hammock inside the gazebo not far from where we stood.

"I win." I chime with breathless glee as he climbs the front steps of the garden house, his boots pounding the wooden planks with every step, and sits me down gently in the hammock.

"Yes, you win! Now let's rest a minute, you spent a lot of magical energy flying that far. I'm quite impressed you made it the entire way." He says taking a seat next to me on the hammock. Cuddling up next to him and gazing up through the glass roof.

"They look so much better out here away from the city. It kind of reminds me of home."

"You never talk about your home." He says offering me a red "candy" ball made from the magical blood of my ancestors.

"Well, I left that life behind me. Anyway, I'm not that girl anymore." I casually say, taking the candy and popping it in my mouth.

"Yes, but you would not be this girl," he says brushing my cheek with his hand, "without that girl. Never forget where you come from and remember to thank the ones who helped you to get there."

"You know somehow you always know just what to say to put things into perspective, but you also sound like a fortune cookie."

"What can I say, I've been around awhile, I know things." He retorts with a boastful grin and charming witty tone, laying back and tucking his hands behind his head like some cocky jock. I scoff at him and roll my eyes but say nothing in hopes it would deflate his ego. Instead, I think his words over and how he truly does always know what to say, sometimes without even knowing the situation that I need advice for. Realizing what I need to do, I excuse myself.

"I think I should make a phone call," before crawling out of the hammock and walking to the edge of the gazebo. I dial the number and stare out to the courtyard, observing the lanterns glow as the phone rings against my ear.

I wait patiently, but it just keeps ringing. I am about to hang up when I hear a voice on the other end of the line pick-up.

"Hello?" The voice says.

"Mama? Hi, it's Jezebel, I know you have been trying to get ahold of me and I have been so busy and everything I haven't had a chance to call you back until now."

"Oh, Jezebel sweetie! I'm so glad you called. I have just arrived in San Francisco as we speak."

"Wait. What!" I said stunned.

"Yes, I have always wanted to visit you in the big city, and you weren't returning my calls. So, I thought that now would be a good time as any. So, I hopped on a plane and am in a cab on my way to your apartment. I wanted to surprise you. Well, Surprise!"

"Surprise," I reply, trying my best to sound convincing but mainly sounding out of breath and bewildered.

"Oh, come on now it will be fun! Oh Darlin', I'm just pullin' up to your building. I'll talk to you in a bit." She says disconnecting the call.

"Mom wait I'm...hello?" I chime in a little too late. "Oh shit!" I quickly dial Ashton's number. Sebastian stands and approaches me swiftly, alarmed. Made aware of my irritation as I started bouncing up and down anxiously, waiting for her to pick up the phone. "Come on. Come on. Answer the phone, Ashton." I say aloud to myself.

"Jezebel, is everything alright?" Sebastian asks in a hushed tone. I am just about to answer him when I suddenly hear Ashton's voice emerge from the device in my hand.

"Hello?" she answers confused by my call.

"Hey! My mom is here in town, and she is on her way up to the apartment but I'm at Sebastian's. I need you to stall her until I can get there."

"How the hell did you get all the way to..."

"We'll discuss it later!" I snap, cutting her off.

"Okay, rawr!" She says imitating a cat sound, "Feisty much? I'm on it, okay?"

"Thank you. Thank you! I will be right there. I love you. Thank you." I yammer on gratefully, completely ignoring the attitude she gave me before hanging up the line. Then I turn to Sebastian who has been waiting patiently for an answer to his question. "I'm so sorry but my…"

"Your mother is here, and you need me to rush us back to your apartment before she notices you are not there."

"Yes, exactly! I just don't think I would be able to make it in time. You are so much faster than I am."

"Wait, say that last part one more time?" He states playfully.

"Sebastian!" I whine ignoring his flirtation, nervous about seeing my mother.

"Alright."

Before I can even respond we are soaring through the sky on the way back to my apartment building. Fifteen minutes or so later we land on the roof and run directly inside the second our feet touch down.

I make it to the apartment door, and I can hear Ashton's subdued voice on the other side giving my mother a tour.

"Over here is the kitchen…" I hear muffled through the door, taking that as our cue to sneak inside and into my bedroom. I begin ripping off my clothes to make the appearance that I had been home more believable.

"Whoa! What are you doing?" Sebastian blurts shocked and shielding his eyes.

"Come on, now is no time for chivalry. Now hand me that towel over there." I screech as I point to the towel hanging off my vanity chair, all while throwing my robe on over my bra and panties. He grabs it and hands it to me swiftly, and I quickly twist it up into my hair.

"Okay, I need you to stay in here."

"Why?" He asks confused, and clearly a little disappointed.

"Because it wasn't that long ago that I broke up with a guy I was supposed to *marry*, and now I'm in my bathrobe and I don't want her to think I'm some kind of hussy."

"Hussy?" He mocks with a grin and a chuckle.

"You know what I mean? We are trying to create the illusion I just got out of the shower not well… something else." He says nothing, just made eyes at me, raising his eyebrows, and biting his bottom lip seductively. Then cracking a sideways grin, he looks me up and down. "Oh, stop that. You know for someone who talks like they are centuries old, sometimes you sure do act like a modern-day guy." Then he sits on my bed somewhat surprised by my comment but looking just as guilty. "Okay, now just please stay in here."

Then speed walking out across the living room to the kitchen. I see Ashton showing my Mother the contents of our refrigerator. Which is humiliatingly mostly full of old takeout boxes.

"Huh, Mama?" I speak up interrupting Ashton's rant about Chinese versus Italian. "Sorry to break up your intriguing conversation on the local cuisine."

"Jezebel, sweetheart." My mother perks up in her wonderful Georgian twang, looking grateful to be saved from the conversation. She approaches me with open arms and wraps me up in a hug, followed by a cheek kiss, "How are you Darlin'?"

"I'm good Mama. It's nice to see you. So, I see you've met my roommate. Ashton this is my mother, Lorraine."

"It is so nice to meet you. I'm also her boss." Ashton adds as she shakes my mother's hand.

My mother shaking her hand in return, noticeably confused by Ashton's random new bit of information. Looking briefly at me and then with an appalled look on her face looks Ashton up and down.

Not surprised by her reaction, considering Ashton is wearing an old Shakira t-shirt that had been cut into a crop top, with no bra, Leaving not much mystery about what was going on up north. Then south of the border, she has on fuzzy cheetah print shorts and white cable knit slipper boots. Her hair is thrown up into the messiest of buns, accessorized by her reading glasses as a headband. All my mother manages to say is, "You write for the newspaper too?"

Trying to move the conversation into less of an awkward topic I chime in by saying, "No, Mama you remember I told you Ashton is one of the directors down at the theatre."

"Oh, so you're in a little play. Isn't that nice? But what do you do for money?"

"Well opening night is this weekend, so hopefully we will do well enough to make up for the deficit."

"What deficit is that Darlin'?"

"Jez quit her day job at the magazine, which paid for a decent portion of our bills until I get my payday. Right now, we are pretty much dependent on what we have in savings. The turnout of the *'little play'* will determine if we need to figure something else out to make it through." There was a moment of stillness while we all glance at each other awkwardly.

Unfortunately, Ashton decides to make a crude joke to break the silence, "Good thing I didn't quit my day job." She says making a little shimming with her chest followed by a little hip-thrusting dance, all while simultaneously symbolizing money by rubbing her fingers together on both hands.

"Okay! Enough talking for you!" I say glaring at Ashton and leading my conservative mother into the living room, away from Ashton's little strip tease. "Let's go in here and catch up, while Ashton makes us a nice cup of tea." Guiding my mother toward the sofa we sit down together.

"So, Mama. How are Daddy and the boys?" I inquire hoping she will take the bait.

"They're good but Hun, but I need you to explain a few things to me. Like why do you live with a hooker? Why did you break up with that nice boy who wanted to marry you? Why did you quit your job? And why do you never come home for visits?"

Feeling a little tense and annoyed by her bluntness I went off, "Well then, let's see that's a lot to unpack. First Ashton is not a *hooker* she was making a joke, a very crude inappropriate joke, but still a joke. Secondly, I broke up with him because he made *me* feel like a *hooker*. My job didn't make me happy anymore and was not worth the torture. I don't come to visit because all you do is question me and tell me how I'm messing up my life. Saying that I'm almost thirty and should be married with kids and a career by now. Well, I already know that Mama, the last thing I need is you reminding me how I'm letting you down."

Then there is nothing but quiet in the room once more. We sit on the couch looking at each other. Waiting to see who would be brave enough to make the next sound. It was so quiet I thought I could hear her eyes blinking like in a cartoon.

"I'll just leave this right here," Ashton says in a hushed tone, placing a tray down on the coffee table. The teapot steaming from its spout and the teacups clinking on their saucers as she sets it down. Then she retreats back to the kitchen, escaping the fog of tension as fast as she can.

"Jezebel," my mother finally speaking up, "I only want to see you have the life I know you deserve." She says the words plainly but with the most delicate tone of love in her voice.

"I know. I'm sorry I blew up like that. But I feel a lot of pressure about your expectations for my life. The thing is, it is *my* life, and I should be allowed to live it how *I* see fit.

Not to live up to your expectation of what is *supposed* to make me happy."

"I try baby girl. I do try to let you live it your way. I just miss you so, you're my only daughter you know. Your brothers don't seem to be in any hurry to give me grandchildren."

"I know. I will try to visit more, I promise." We both smile at each other and embrace in a much-needed hug. Feeling so secure in finally having spoken up and sharing feelings I've been trying to communicate for the past nine years. "Would you like some tea?" I ask politely.

"Sure Hun. So, do you have a new fella yet?" Momma inquires politely, seemingly continuing her train of thought about grandchildren.

"Yes, she does. His name is Sebastian, and he is so hot," Ashton states entering the room now that the coast is clear of any more harshly spoken words between relatives.

"Thanks," I say plainly while giving her a blatant stare, trying to make my dislike for her overstep a little obvious.

"Well, I can't wait to meet him," Mama says excitingly moving the conversation along. I give her my best convincing smile and sip my tea.

"Me too, actually he is coming to the play, why don't I reserve a ticket for you, and you can meet him then," Ashton says obviously not picking up my subtle hints of attitude.

"Oh, that would be wonderful Darlin'. I can't wait!" Mother states gleefully, with a genuine ear-to-ear grin.

We continue the rest of the night discussing general small talk and catching up. Then we set up the sofa bed for my mother and all say our goodnights. I then open the door of my bedroom to find Sebastian poking through my dresser.

"What are you doing?" I say a little surprised by the invasion of my privacy.

"Nothing!" He blurted back, swiftly tucking everything away, closing the drawers and finally turning to face me.

"Really? Snooping? That is so beneath you Sebastian." I say with a hint of disappointment in my voice.

"I got bored." He responds under his breath, defending himself. I say nothing, just flash him a judgmental look as I sit on my bed.

"So, how was your visit with your mother?" He inquires, changing the subject. Trying his best to evade my harsh stare of conviction, as he sits next to me on the bed.

"It was good. The conversation was more brief than I thought it would be. It came out a lot easier than I thought but we finally cleared the air on some personal matters. Oh, and she wants to meet you." I finally say, before getting up and getting dressed for bed.

I take off my robe and slip on a nightgown, as I pull it down, I look up to see him gawking at me. As he catches me looking in his direction, he quickly averts his gaze, attempting to conceal the fact that he was just caught staring at me. At that moment, a smile slowly spreads across my face.

"Are you gonna stay the night?" I ponder, as I crawl into bed.

"Is that an invitation?"

"No, but it would probably be easier than trying to sneak you past my sleeping mother."

"Agreed. I know we discussed you staying with me, but your mother is here so it's probably best you sleep in your own bed tonight."

"Oh, that's right, I'm so sorry Sebastian I didn't know she was co…"

Then he cuts me off by holding up his hand and saying, "No. I understand you are safe as long as you are here. Just whatever you do, do not remove your amulet. I will be here till you fall asleep." Then he gives me a final kiss before we turn out the lights. We snuggled closer in bed, and I felt so secure falling asleep in his arms for the second night in a row. I can get used to this I think to myself before drifting away into a deep slumber.

Chapter 5
Sebastian

STANDING OVER HER AS SHE SLEEPS IN HER bed, her existence is so peaceful and beautiful. I check to see if she has her amulet on before softly kissing her cheek and making my exit. I exit her apartment and stalk down the hall, writing her a text to see first thing in the morning.

Good morning my love I am excited for the opening of the play this weekend. However, if I am going to be able to attend, I need to finish up some paperwork. Have a good day with your mother. Love -SB.

I send the text just as I step on the elevator to the roof; I fly back to the manor with only one thing on my mind. The thoughts race through my mind as I ponder why Thaddeus is suddenly here. Landing in front of the house I fold my wings away. Then I head straight to my office, trying to put all supernatural matters aside and focus on my work. While I am sitting at my desk finishing up all my paperwork, I hear Jasper's coarse voice from the doorway.

"There you are Little Bat." He says my childhood nickname as he approaches the desk.

"Hello there old man." I tease back, looking up from some forms to meet his gaze.

"I see Miss Jones isn't joining us tonight." He says while placing a goblet on the desk gently so as not to spill the red liquid inside.

"No, her mother is here for a visit and so I escorted her home. Besides, I need to finish some work before this weekend. Jezebel has invited me to the opening night of the play. I have a lot of papers to sign and preparations to get done if they are going to be able to perform. The theatre needs me to sign so many new policies and insurance forms for this play, so it must be good. Not to mention I have to put together the payroll before opening night." Rambling on, it became evident that none of my words were resonating with him.

"Are you sure Master Thaddeus, won't be able to make any trouble while you are separated? You know the manor is the safest place for her, even with the protection of the Sapphire, she is not completely hidden."

"Jasper please, I am not a little boy anymore..." I growl before pausing and taking a quick breath to clear my head before completely exploding on him. "My apologies. I know, but I'm sure wherever Thad is hiding. He has yet to discover her residence."

"He found her place of work without you knowing about it, and she has only just begun working at the theatre."

"Well, he probably has his Gýmona to thank for that, it knows her scent. It found her in the parking garage… of her apartment building." As the thoughts came back to me, I realized what a mistake I had made leaving her there alone. I had completely forgotten about the beast. I quickly pick up my phone and pace back and forth frantically as it rings.

"Hello." I hear Jezebel's sleepy voice say through the phone.

"Jezebel, you have to leave your apartment right now!" I shout urgently.

"What? Why? Who is this?" She responds while still half asleep.

"It is Sebastian. Jezebel, get the hell out of there! You are in danger!"

"Sebastian, what do you mean?" she asks a little more awake, picking up on the demanding tone in my voice. "In danger how?"

"I will explain it to you later, but if you want Ashton and your Mother alive when the sun rises you must to leave the apartment now!"

"Okay, I'm heading out the door right now." I hear rustling on the other end of the phone and a door shut. Then speaking up again she says, "I'll be at the mansion soon." The line goes dead, as she has disconnected the call.

"Jezebel?" I say frantically into the phone, surprised by the abrupt cut-off of communication. "No. No. No, no, no. Jezebel!"

I slam the phone down on the desk and sped toward the door, past Jasper who is still standing in my office. I make my way through the house and back to the courtyard. Standing in the middle of the maze I scan the heavens for her. "Where is she?" I think aloud, not taking my eyes off the night sky.

"Lost something, have you?" I hear a familiar voice say from in the darkness of the night. I scan the darkness of the night, looking around until I see him. He is perching like a gargoyle on the peak of the fountain that stands erect in the center of the courtyard, not but a few yards from where I am standing.

"You again?" I growl.

"Who me?" He jests with a conniving grin followed by a maniacal laugh. "You didn't honestly think that rooftop would be the last you'd see of me, did you? Bastian you know I'm harder to dispose of than that or had you forgotten."

"What do you want Thad?" I press slowly making my way towards him still perched on the fountain.

"I told you. I. Want. The. Girl." He says plainly.

"Well, she does not want you."

"Aww, ain't that cute. Bastian's *wittle feewings* are still hurt cause the other half of his 'star-bound soul' chose me." He taunts.

"She would never!" I growl once more as I hasten my speed to a full sprint in his direction. The loose gravel crunching and kicking up dust beneath my feet as I move. Then launching myself through the air, I fly at him like a bullet. My arms stretching out in front of me, my strong hands ready to tighten around his scrawny neck. However, just as I am about to grab onto him, he disappears into a puff of smoke, literally slipping through my fingers. I continue to soar through the air, so I initiate my dismount. Landing with a quick tuck, roll, and pivot I return to my feet. I desperately search the blackness of the garden for any sign of his whereabouts, trying to decipher where he might have vanished.

I hear only the sounds of the night; the wind rustling in the foliage, crickets, and a nearby dove. Then instantaneously there is a rustling in the bushes, so I turn to catch him but see nothing except the emptiness of the courtyard. Not long after, from behind me, I hear his dreaded laughter, echoing on the breeze, as if we were children again playing hide and seek. Only this time the stakes are higher, and we are no longer children playing games. We are enemies at war.

"Enough Thad!" I roar ferociously, quickly running out of patience for him.

"You never did win a single match we played, did you?"

I turn to see him standing just behind me, but before I could make a single move. I am blast in the face with a powerful blow from his fist, knocking me to the ground.

"That's because you always cheated." I choke out the words, still trying to catch my breath. Rolling over on the gravel as I recover from sucker punch.

"Yet, I still got the girl, didn't I?" He states with a laugh. Obviously to himself but loud enough for me to hear, as he walks aimlessly around the yard.

"More like *stole* the girl," I say as I climb to my feet, fiercely glaring into his yellow snake eyes.

"I am no cheater; I am only playing the game that you started." He says crouching into an attack stance. I mirror his actions ready to fight him again, but then I am distracted by a sound.

"Sebastian!" I hear a voice call from the skies. I look up to see Jezebel flying over the manor. Then quickly look back to where Thad had been to find him gone.

"Jezebel!" I shout to her as she starts to descend. I began running, my arms spread as if to catch her.

"What is going on?" She pleads as she touches down on the gravel, just in time for me to wrap my arms around her. Stunned by her reaction because she did not return my affections, but I hold her tightly still. Thankful to have warned her in time.

"Uh, Sebastian!" Jezebel states shakingly, trying to get my attention.

"What?" I ask before finally loosening my hold on her. I then see her pointing across the courtyard toward the gazebo. I turn around to find Thad standing there with the Gýmona. Petting the creature as if it were a labradoodle and not a vicious beast.

"Hey Lover-boy, I brought a friend too. Meet my new pet, Duchess." Thad boasts proudly about his new companion.

"That thing is a female!" Jezebel blurts in disgust, obviously not meaning to do so out loud because she covers her mouth instantly after. Offended by her comment the Gýmona snarls ferociously and begins speeding toward both of us.

"Well look what you started. You pissed her off!" I bellow as we escape toward the house.

"I didn't mean to!" She responds horrified as we continue our mad dash toward the rear entrance. Approaching the doors of the manor, then sliding to an unexpected halt, as Thaddeus is standing in the way of our escape.

"Going somewhere, were you?" He inquires in the cocky way he says most things. "I didn't think so. She is coming with me." Pointing to Jezebel and then holding out his hand as if waiting for me to hand her over. Instead, I tuck her behind me.

Jezebel and I stand back-to-back, both crouching in a staggered stance. Trapped between the beast and his pet trying not to make any sudden moves.

"Why do you want me to come with you so bad?" Jezebel inquires. He just looks at her confused, then he looks at me with a smirk and says, "You haven't told her yet, have you?"

"Told me what?" I hear her say, shortly after there is a booming of thunder followed by a flash of lightning and it starts to rain. The sudden downpour of water causes the Gýmona to cower away, whimpering. We watch as it scampers into the darkness disappearing from our sight. Then we both stand up straight and glare at Thaddeus.

"Argh, no!" He roars disappointed by the retreating of his pet, the rain making holes in his smokey appearance.

"Oh, does big boy Thad miss his ugly doggy? He is all alone and outnumbered now." Jezebel teases Thad in a baby voice, obviously pissing him off.

"I will have you for myself before the Halo Moon. You can bet your life on it." Thaddeus threatens directly to Jezebel before completely evaporating into a puff of smoke and blowing away in the breeze.

"What the fuck just happened!" Jezebel affirms in my direction. I sigh because I did not know her *that* well yet, but I knew enough to know she only curses when she has met the peak of her patience. She needs to know more about our history anyway. I hoped it could wait until after the play, but things seem to be moving faster and there are too many factors out of my control. So, I take this as a sign that I need to do so sooner than I had planned.

"Come inside please," I say feeling defeated, stepping firmly as I walk passed her and opening the French doors of the manor, "we will talk." I hear her footsteps following along behind me. We walk through the manor dripping wet from the pouring rain, both our feet squishing with each step.

"Why did you call me here Sebastian?" She inquires, still dazed by the sudden events that woke her just moments ago.

"I'm sorry, but I was talking with Jasper, and he reminded me of when you told me about the Gýmona in your parking garage. Meaning it knows where you live and so it could lead Thaddeus there. In an effort to protect you, and by extension your mother and Ashton, I needed you to return to the manor immediately."

"Oh, my goddess! He wouldn't hurt them, would he?" she inquires with understandable fear and worry in her voice.

"I do not think so. What he really wants is you and you are here. However, had I known he was here when I called you, I probably would have told you to stay put."

"No, I am glad you called me. I feel better knowing I can keep him away from my family if I am here. Besides, it sounds like you have another history lesson for me?"

"Something like that." I chortle at her comment as we finally make it upstairs to my bedroom door. I open the door and step aside so she can enter.

"What are we doing here?" She asks, confused.

"I think it's important you finish getting a good night's rest before we tackle your 'history lesson'."

"Now that I hear you say it, you are probably right." She says in agreeance as she approaches me and gives me a soggy peck on the cheek.

I ring the bell and have Eliza bring Jezebel some dry clothes. I turn to hand her the garments to find she is sitting by the fire warming up. I hand her the dry pajamas and then enter my bed chamber to do the same.

I have just finished pulling my shirt over my head when I see she is standing in the threshold, entangled in the velvet curtains. I smile at her as so tiptoes into the room. Scurrying her way to the bed, pulling back the blankets, and crawling in. She turns to see I am still standing by the doorway.

"Aren't you going to join me?" she asks confused by my stand-offish behavior.

"I did not get a chance to finish my meal and am feeling a little…"

"Say no more, please go eat. I will be here when you are ready." She says as she makes herself more comfortable in my bed.

"I will return shortly." I turn to exit, pause, then turn back. I approach the side of the bed and sit just next to her on the edge of the mattress.

"Jezebel?" I speak softly, looking into her eyes adoringly.

"Yes, Sebastian?" She responds by batting her eyes at me flirtatiously.

"I would briefly like to take a moment to say, I have truly enjoyed having you here in my home. I did not realize how much I had gotten used to being alone until I had you here with me."

"I like it too; you make me feel safe. I am falling for you so fast that I can hardly catch my breath. If it weren't for all the supernatural distractions. I think I would lose myself in your beautiful amber eyes." I say nothing in response, feeling blown away by her boldness. I just lean in and kiss her passionately; she reciprocates my affections. Feeling the rush of the frenzy building up inside me, I suddenly push her away. Walk swiftly away from the bed I stand frozen as I continue the ongoing internal brawl with my inner demons.

"Hey, what is the matter?" I hear her sweet voice ask from the bed behind me, concerned. Holding my hands over my mouth to hide my fangs, not knowing how to admit to her what just happen.

So instead, with my back still turned away, over my shoulder I say firmly, "Nothing, goodnight," rushing out of the room. Trying hard to avoid thinking of the event, I push it out of my mind entirely, and I head down to the kitchen. I enter the dining room to find Jasper standing at the table polishing the silver.

"Are we having guests?" I ask puzzled, not realizing we still owned silver.

"Yes, I thought it would be nice to invite Jezebel and her mother to dinner tomorrow evening."

"That is a swell idea, Jasper. Thank you. I will be sure to mention it to her in the morning." I state impressed by his initiative. I then begin looking around the room. I didn't get too far before I hear the old man pipe up again.

"It is in the kitchen Little Bat." He says with a grin, but not taking his eyes off the spoon he was shining. I did not say anything in response, I just smile and let out a little chuckle, comfort to have had him taking care of me my whole life.

Then I quickly escape into the kitchen and there on the counter is the goblet of fresh blood that Jasper had brought me in the office. I guzzle it down as fast as I can and just as I am about finished with the last swallow, the door of the kitchen opens. Still not lowering the cup from my lips I look over to see who has come in. Jezebel is standing there in the doorway with a disturbed look on her face.

"Would you two like to be alone together?" She teases, obviously a little freaked out by the display she has walked in on yet again and trying to break the ice. I drop the cup from my mouth and wipe the corners of my lips with my fingers, flashing her a cheesy smile of humiliation.

"Okay, since I'm apparently going to be the only one doing the talking, I guess I'll just say it. Do I really make you that hungry?" she asks, wasting no time with small talk.

My expression immediately changes, as I am caught off guard by her sensual implication. So, I turn away and place the goblet down on the counter. I sigh dumbfounded, I quickly try to collect my thoughts, after my head is done reeling. I turn to face her, to find she is now directly in front of me.

"I was starting to get swept up in the moment. I didn't want my hunger to get the best of me and hurt you." I finally say, my eyes drifting as I try avoiding eye contact, ashamed of my nature. She just giggles, confused I look at her, shocked by her reaction. "Why is that funny?" I ask still feeling adrift by the entire interaction.

"Sebastian, I have a confession to make." She says pouting her lips but in a sensual voice, as she slowly caresses my face with her fingertips. Tracing my cheekbone, grazing my lips gently, tracking them down my neck stopping at my sternum.

"Yes?" I respond, getting more confused by the minute but also feeling so aroused by her sudden sensuality.

"I know I jumped up and made a big scene about when you bit me before," she says, firmly placing her arms around my waist and leaning in. Stunned, I try to make a getaway, but I am being pinned against the counter. So, I tense up and the only action I can manage is to lean backward. Then she continues talking in the same sexy whisper. This time directly into my ear, "To be honest with you, I actually kind of liked it."

She whispers before nipping at my earlobe, grazing the skin on my neck with her teeth, and giggling again. My skin is electrified by her touch. However, I am still astonished, so I stand frozen and tense. The feeling of her teeth on my neck causes the frenzy to rise, my body is trembling at the idea of tasting her again.

Unable to resist the thought my eyes start to wonder, finding her buttery skin glistening, as her nightgown strap falls from her shoulder exposing her collar bone.

"Oops," she says playfully, as she catches the strap but tilts her head to the side, exposing her neck. Being unable to resist my inner animal, I feel my fangs peeking out from behind my lips. I see her kinky grin at the sight of them. After first taking a deep breath, I plunge them into her neck. Infatuated by the moment I grab her body and pull it into mine until our hips meet. Feeling so engrossed in the moment I start to lose myself in the blood, and then I hear her moan seductively, bringing my mind back to reality. Having only tasted her briefly before releasing my grip and letting her go completely.

"There is more where that came from Big Boy." She says temptingly before fixing her gown and all at once disappearing from the room, blood still leaking from her neck. I try to catch my mind up realizing what had just happened, not quite sure how to feel about it. After regaining control of my faculties, I quickly follow her out the kitchen door. She is nowhere to be found; I return to my room to find her lying in bed with the lights out.

"Jezebel?" I call out to her but there is no answer, she is fast asleep. I approach the bed to find her sleeping peacefully, so I give her a soft kiss on the lips and leave the room.

I sit in the foyer flipping through the pages of *The Book of Demons* while petting the cat, who sits just next to me on the sofa. My mind throbbing as I start thinking about how I would tell Jezebel the rest of the story; wondering how she would take it. Hoping it would not make her run again.

The only way to be sure is to follow through when the sun comes up.

Then to ease my troubled mind, I begin reminiscing about the scandal in the kitchen just moments ago. Her sensual walk, and the grazing of her teeth on my skin. I had bitten many before, but this was the first time I myself had ever been bitten. Granted she does not have fangs like I do, but it was thrilling just the same.

And the taste of her delectable life force, the warmth of her blood on my tongue was enough to make me ravenous. I smile with the fleeting memory stirring in my mind feeling my blood beginning to rush, grabbing at my neck where she had nibbled. Tracing the spot with my fingers as if her teeth never left my skin. Astonished by the sheer pleasure I felt. Thinking our relationship is heading in the right direction.

Chapter 6
Jezebel

O PENING MY EYES TO FIND THE SUN'S rays shining in the room. I smile at the beautiful beam as it warms my skin. Then I see the red curtains hanging on the bedpost just inches from the window and quickly realize that I am in Sebastian's bed.

"Sebastian?" I wail, flailing my body upright, tears starting to form in my eyes at the empty response. Looking around to see I am alone in the bed; I swiftly run into the foyer of his room. Tearing through the curtains that separate the bed chamber, finding it also to be empty. This causes the cold tears to fall from my eyes. "Sebastian! Answer me!" I scream once more, tears streaming heavily as I run into the hall toward the main part of the house. Searching frantically for any sign of him, terrified, my mind begins to assume the worst.

Had he been lying next to me as I slept? Did he not notice the open curtains? Did he burn up as the sun rose and I didn't even notice? Or did Thad have something to do with this? Just as the last thought rolled into my mind and my heart began cracking in half, I hear a voice.

"Jezebel?" The voice says in confusion of my frantic state. I turn to see Sebastian standing in the middle of the hall. Relieved to see him alive, I run to him and wrap him firmly in my arms.

Confused by this but still holding on to me he asks, "Jezebel, what is the matter?" Then through tear-soaked eyes and a runny nose, I answer the best I can manage.

"I woke up, and the sun was shining in the room, and I didn't know if you were alive." The tears begin to run down my face again just thinking about the words I was saying. So, I tighten my grip around his waist as I softly sob into his chest.

"Oh, Jezebel. My sweet. It was I who opened the curtains for you so you would not sleep too long. I apologize for the scare but do not worry I have been in the main foyer waiting for you to wake." he says with compassion but under a wide grin and a bit of a chuckle.

"You think this is funny?" I utter feeling perturbed, pushing away from him. I wipe the tears from my face and glare at him feeling hurt that this event made him laugh.

"No. I do not think it is funny. I think you are sweet." He says trying to clarify, but ultimately letting out another chuckle. I could also see he was doing his best to choke down yet more laughter.

"Why are you laughing?" I shout fighting through his contagious smile, trying to stay serious to let him know I am upset. He says nothing, just give me an even wider smirk causing me to smile back. Which set him off entirely as he burst into a full-on laugh fest. Then I start to giggle which makes me even more furious. I began to lightly hit him on the arm.

"Why? Are? You? Laughing?" I speak each word aloud in rhythm with every strike to his body, "I am serious!"

"I just love knowing you were genuinely concerned for my safety, it is adorable." He says through his explosive laughter, causing my face to beam a bright blush and fight through the smile I felt forming on my face. I am flattered by his comment, but I did not want him to know it, so instead I try to stay serious and defend my position.

"It is not." I squeal, feeling the butterflies tickle my stomach, and losing the battle with my facial muscles I too flashed an ear-to-ear grin. Which only made him laugh harder.

"See how cute you are." He teases, as he looks at me and continues to laugh, trying to get me to laugh with him. I did my best to stay firm and would not allow him to break me. Then he suddenly starts to tickle me, causing me to fall to the ground and burst into laughter. He follows me to the ground and continues to tickle my sides.

"That is cheating!" I shout through the excitement and the tingles I felt all over my body. "Okay stop, you win. You win. I give!" I scream, pleading with him to stop. We were lying on the ground laughing when we felt a presence standing over us.

"If you are quite finished, I have the car ready for Miss Jones," Jasper says seemingly unamused by out childlike behavior. We both immediately stand up and avoid eye contact with Jasper. Feeling embarrassed to be two full grown adults having been caught tangled in a tickle fest, in the middle of the hallway no less.

"I will just go get dressed." I say, still avoiding eye contact with Jasper and sneaking away from the awkwardness of the moment. But not completely disappearing before glancing back at Sebastian with a smile to find him smiling back at me.

I enter my room and begin my normal morning routine. After changing my clothes, I realize I couldn't find my phone. Then I remember I left it in Sebastian's bed chamber. So, I head to his room. As I approach the newly made bed, I see that the black cat I had met the prior day, is napping on the bed. I stood looking at his peaceful state when I notice something strange about him, he is glowing. There is a golden-yellow mist around him, and he looks almost transparent.

Then suddenly I see a glowing hand stroking the small creature, looking up only to be aghast by what my eyes saw. I am looking at me, there on the other side of the bed, is my spitting image. However, based on her attire I realize it wasn't me but Brigitta. She sits on the bed glowing with the same golden hues as the cat; it is like looking at a ghost. Dressed in a beautiful flowing gown, with ruffle accents on the sleeves and collar. She begins to speak; her voice is hollow causing the words to sound like a muffled echo.

Then her voice comes into focus, and I hear her say, "Oh, my sweet Blink. What do you think I should tell Sebastian about Thad? He would be devastated if he knew I am with child." She spoke to the black feline curled up on the bed, still napping. She finishes petting the cat, grabs a book off the side table, and walks around the bed right toward me. Not knowing what to do, I freeze but she continues to walk right through me leaving a trail of golden mist in her wake. I turn around and follow her to the foyer. Standing in the doorway that separates the foyer and the bed chamber I watch her. Her movements seem almost like a dance as she sways and fades through the air. Then standing in front of the fireplace flipping through the pages of her book. She grabs a quill off the mantle, sits, and writes in the book.

"It's a journal," I whisper aloud to myself as I watch the vision, Briggita continues to write.

Then the vision fades away and shifts, suddenly a man and woman appear on the sofa. It is the same Briggita but now she is with Sebastian, he is wearing a loose white shirt and tight black trousers. They began to talk and share a laugh, once more everything sounding like a hollow, muffled echo. Then I see them lean in for a kiss but just as their lips meet, they evaporate into a cloud of golden mist and then nothing at all. Then my phone buzzes on the nightstand causing me to jump out of my skin, I swiftly pick up the small device.

Then the real cat runs out from under the bed scaring me for a second time. I squeal as he runs past me through the doorway; Sebastian enters the room as the cat exits.

"Sorry about that. I don't know what could have startled the little guy. His name is…"

"Blink," I say interrupting him, then he looks at me stunned.

"How did you know that?" Sebastian asks, still looking surprised.

"Well, I saw," I begin as I simultaneously check my phone, seeing a new text from Ashton that read.

'Where are you? Rehearsals have already begun.'

"Oh shit! Sorry, Sabastian I'll have to explain later I really need to go." I yammer off quickly, then I run past him and head for the door. Then I double back around giving him a quick kiss before continuing out the door, through the mansion, and out to the car that Jasper still had waiting for me outside.

We drive up to the Theatre, I thank Jasper for the ride, and jump out of the car. I enter the auditorium to find everyone already on stage in costume and Ashton standing with her stage manager in the first row of seats. She turns to face me as I come running down the aisle.

"Nice of you to join us." Ashton says in a haughty tone, "No need to get into costume we don't have time to wait for you."

"Sorry Ash. I had a *personal* emergency." I say as I stop at the end of the row, she is in. Trying to tell her in code about my witchy moment. She looks at me like she is trying to decode my message.

Then she approaches me saying, "You mean like a voodoo thing?" she mumbles between clenched teeth.

"Yes, and I wish you would stop using that word." I hiss back.

"Gotcha." She whispers with a single nod. Then pivoting back around she continues, "Well, you're here now so let's continue." Ashton says aloud for everyone to hear while walking back to her previous spot in the front row.

I jump on stage and the other actors continue from where they had stopped, I look to Ashton and mouth the words, "Thank you." She grins at me and gives me a quick wink before drawing her attention back to the scene.

Flipping through the pages of my script to make sure I have all my blocking and lines down before going out on stage. As I am waiting at stage right for my cue my phone buzzes. I take it out to see a text from Sebastian.

'Hello, my dear, Jasper has put together a dinner for you and your mother tonight. Feel free to bring anyone else you would like to join us. Please come formally dressed. PS I enjoyed our rendezvous in the kitchen last night as well as the fun in the hall this morning. Again, my apologies for the curtain mishap. -SB'

I smile at the text, but also feel a little confused about some of its contents. Even still I text back, *'That sounds wonderful I will let them know.'* punctuating my text with lots of heart and kissy face emojis. I respond only to the first part of the text and ponder what to say about the second half. Confused by what moment in the kitchen he could be referring to.

Then I notice my cue coming up, so I switch my phone to silent. Then I slip it in my pocket just in time for me to go onstage. Rehearsing the entire play three times, before we all gather at the front of the stage for a cast meeting, just like we do every day.

"Okay everyone," Ashton begins her director's spiel. "Everything is looking great. So, we are gonna take tomorrow off. Don't want to overwork ourselves before the show this weekend. Everyone please get plenty of rest, go over your lines and remember…"

"Drink plenty of water!" The entire cast says in unison interrupting her monologue and mocking her daily speech. Then the entire auditorium erupts with laughter.

Ashton standing with a grin, humbled, and embarrassed by the taunting but participating in the humor.

"Okay, okay get out of here. I will see you all in two days. Please everyone show up six hours before showtime for wardrobe and makeup. And to all my crew members please show up three hours before showtime, except for you select few. You know who you are." Then the group of actors disperses and heads backstage to de-robe.

I walk over to Ashton ready to go, not needing to *'de-robe'*. I approach her from behind and am just about to tap her on the shoulder when she turns around and starts rambling.

"How could you leave me alone with your mother this morning? I had to eat breakfast with the woman. Have you ever eaten breakfast with your mother? It is awkward. Also, where did you sneak off to anyway?"

"We'll talk in the car?" I respond by making light of her complaints and trying to keep quiet on anything *'witch'* related in public areas.

"Well then let's go." She says firmly as we collect her things and head toward the door. I trail along behind her to her car which is parked on the side of the building.

We drove home in silence for just a couple of blocks before she broke the silence.

"Well, go on! Tell me what happened."

"Umm, okay I guess I should catch you up. So, there is this guy, and Sebastian figured out last night that he knows where we live so to keep you and Mama safe, I had to leave the apartment in the middle of the night. He's also the reason I had to ditch our double date the other day. I am kind of freaking out about it. Sebastian is supposed to tell me more. Which reminds me could you please take me to his place instead of home?"

"Sure. I have never seen his house and you haven't talked much about it either. Even though you're there like all the time!" She agrees excitingly, completely ignoring everything else I said but instead of trying to repeat myself, I just let it be. I instruct her in the direction of Sebastian's house, leaving the city and entering the more rural part of San Francisco.

"I have lived here for years and I have yet to see this part of the city. Are we even still in San Francisco?" She asks. However, I am preoccupied with navigating so I didn't respond. We drive the rest of the way in silence, enjoying the scenery and openness of being separated from the concrete jungle of the city.

"Turn here," I instruct as we approach the gates of the manor.

"Sebastian lives here?" she retorts rhetorically, being blown away by the huge mansion at the end of the gravel driveway. Then we walk up the stairs to the front door and Jasper is already waiting for me, or us rather.

"Thanks, Jasper," I say casually.

"What a cute little butler dude." Ashton mocks impolitely as Jasper takes Ashton's coat. I roll my eyes and scoff at her comment. Doing my best to brush off the awkwardness of her behavior.

"Please excuse her Jasper, she is not used to such hospitality," I say defending her and trying to clear the air.

"Quite alright Miss Jones, however I believe an introduction is needed."

"Oh right, this is my roommate Ashton. Ashton this is Jasper, he is Sebastian's uh, well he's…" I stammer not knowing exactly what his title is considering he does so many different jobs.

"He is my manservant, but mostly he is an old family friend," Sebastian says entering the room, already half-dressed in his fancy clothes. Happy to be seeing him again I approach him, and he welcomes me by wrapping me up tightly in his arms and kissing me keenly. "Hello, my love!" He says to me sweetly before addressing the room, "I thought I heard voices. Hello Ashton, nice to see you again. Welcome to my home."

"It's a beautiful home. I had no idea that this was where Jezebel was escaping. I understand her not wanting to come back to our small apartment when she gets to experience all this."

"Well thank you." He responds politely and then turns his attention to Jasper. "Jasper, could you please fetch our guests some beverages as well as something to nibble? We will be in the parlor."

"Right away sir," Jasper says, bowing his head and exiting the room toward the kitchen.

Then everyone moves from the entryway and walks slowly into the parlor.

"Where is your mother, she is our guest of honor." Sebastian inquires.

"Oh, we just got off work. Honestly, I had forgotten to tell Ashton and Mama about dinner. Sorry."

"No bother, dinner is not for a while yet. So, we shall have refreshments and then you can pick her up later." He says casually as if this sort of thing happened to him all the time.

We enter the parlor just as one of the servants finishes lighting the fireplace. Everyone gathers around the coffee table. We sit in awkward silence for what seems like forever but what is mostly like only five or ten minutes. The only sound is the roar of the fire. Then Jasper comes in with a trolley, squeaking as it rolls into the silence of the room. He places a tray of snacks on the coffee table, as well as some empty glasses and a pitcher of iced tea.

"Will there be anything else sir?" Jasper respectfully asks Sebastian and waits patiently for a response.

"No, thank you, Jasper. That will be all," he says, dismissing Jasper from the room with a wave of his hand. I watch as Jasper exits the room and then I pour the iced tea.

"Would you like some?" I ask Ashton politely, offering her a glass.

"No, why don't you give it to Sebastian. I'm sure he's thirsty." Then realizing what she might have insinuated she gets flustered and chokes on her words. "No, I didn't mean thirsty, as in like *thirsty*. I...I meant you know like...hungry for some liquids. Oh, no. No that didn't come out right either."

"Ashton!" I state under my breath, getting her attention.

"What?" She responds nervously.

"It's alright. Breathe." I say serenely, in an effort to comfort my babbling friend.

"Thanks for the offer though," Sebastian teases with a chuckle. "It is always quite humorous for me to make you mortals uncomfortable. Considering I do often '*hunger for liquids.*' He says slightly embarrassed but trying hard to bury it under a façade of confidence.

"Glad I amuse you," Ashton says mockingly with a grin, taking her glass of tea and sipping it red-faced and mortified.

"Well then, now that we have dealt with the awkward elephant in the room or vampire I guess. Ashton, it was lovely to have you. Thanks for dropping me off. Why don't you head on home?"

"And spend the night alone with your kooky mother. I don't think so. Not going through that again." She replies still steaming from her morainic episode.

"Actually, you and Mama have been invited for dinner tonight. So, you need to go get dressed; something classy, and pick up Mama."

"Okay, when you say class do you mean like..." Then cutting her off before she had time to spout any more obscenities I say, "Like wedding classy, not club classy."

"What?" she inquires, seeming puzzled by my comparisons.

"Think runway," I state, trying my best to paint a picture for her.

"Ah, gotcha! Okay, I shall be back." She responds enthusiastically, chugging the rest of her tea, grabbing some snacks from the tray, and stuffing them in her purse. Then strolling her way out of the room.

"Thanks. You're the best!" I shout after her.

"Whatever. Love ya." I hear her call back before hearing the front door to the manor shut with an echo in the main hall.

Then wasting no time, I turn to Sebastian and say, "Okay we have from now until they return for you to give me a crash course on everything you have left to teach me."

"Well let's not waste a single second. Take my hand." He responds, holding out his hand for me to grab it. Feeling confident as to what would happen if I did, I took his hand. Instantaneously we start whooshing through the air, making it difficult for me to focus on any one object, as everything in the manor blurs by in a haze of color.

Then we suddenly come to a halt, now standing in front of the secret bookcase entrance that hides the Sacred Study.

"Can I do it, Sebastian? I never get to open the doorway."

"Of course, you may. This room is more for you than me. You know you being the witch in this coupling." He spoke.

I reach my hand back into the bookcase to press the button that opens the door. The bookcase sinks back into the wall and then slides out of the way with a rough grating sound, revealing the doorway.

"That never gets old. Although for being a magic room, you would think there would be a more magical way to get in." I say as we walk into the Altar Room and approach the door of the Sacred Study.

"Oh, there used to be but when I no longer had anyone around with magic, I had to figure out another way. Bless the technologies of this realm." He jokes whilst opening the door to the study, just on the other side of the Alter Room.

"Okay let me find my bearing." He says, searching the many bookcases and drawers of the room. I sit patiently at the table, preparing my mind mentally for everything he is about to tell me. Staring up at the giant painting of Briggita I knew that some of it would be hard to hear.

Confident that it was my destiny, and that I would be able to follow through. I would be the witch I was born to be and nothing could stop me. I am done running scared and playing games. I have come to terms with the fact that I will never be the girl I was before Sebastian. That girl was lost and afraid. I am Jezebel Selene Jones, and I am a badass witch!

Chapter 7
Sebastian

AFTER MAKING OUR WAY UP TO THE Sacred Study, Jezebel waits patiently at the table as I rummage about the room. I search through books and papers, gathering all the materials I will need to explain what I have to say.

I can tell the difference between the girl I met at the concert and the one sitting here before me. She is not only more confident and capable with her magic, but she seems to enjoy herself. She is not as afraid or insecure of this world as she was when I first introduced it to her. *Granted I'm sure being assaulted by a vampire on your first date probably is not ideal; especially when that vampire is your date.*

This makes me feel more at ease, knowing that she is open to the conversation. My fear that she would run starts to subside. When I am sure I have everything, I sit on the opposite side of the table.

"So, do you remember the tale I told you about our two covens first coming together?" She nods in response and glances down at the wax tapestries I had shown her before, still laid out on the table. "Well, there is a little more you need to know if you are to truly understand our destined path."

"Whatever it is Sebastian, tell me. I am ready."

"Okay, first there is something I need to tell you about Thaddeus. When we were boys, we were best friends, we did everything together. We spent every day running through the halls of the castle causing mischief or out in the stables tending to the horses. We even attended the same lessons in education and combat. We were inseparable, true allies."

"What happened? Cause the exchanges I've seen between you guys have been anything but friendly."

"Well, there is something that even he doesn't know. Something I have been hiding from him long before our feud began. He is not just my comrade; he is my half-brother." I say modestly, standing up and laying out a scroll of my family tree on the table in front of her.

"Wait, what?" she says stunned, as she scans the huge parchment that is now in front of her.

"So, you know there have been four reaping's of your soul. Malishca being the very first of the *Steorra Erastés*; translation *'the Star Lovers'*."

"Is that really what we are called?" she asks with an unimpressed giggle.

"Yes, in the history books, we are known as the *Steorra Erastés*," I say, giving her a loving grin, and a wink.

Then continuing from my brief tangent, "Do you remember the story of Malishca? Full name Malishca Verena Bronwyn Sanballet." I recite as I point to the scroll of her family tree.

"Yes, she was my ancestor, or me, I guess. She is the reason for this whole, star lover's thing, in the first place." She replies with a hint of sass, "You never really explained the reason why Malishca was recycled."

"She was found fornicating with her former lover after she had been bonded to the Vampire prince." I sum up abruptly.

"Are you kidding me?" She scoffs in disappointment.

"That's the story, she had been engaged to him in secret before she got sick, and then the bargaining of souls was created to save her life. I guess her love for him never faded. So, the Fates came and took her soul to be recycled but not before she bore a child. Thus, continuing your ancestry. So not all bad news, without it you would not be here."

"So just because she was bound to the Vampire Prince, didn't mean she had to love him."

"No, it doesn't work like that. I mean I'm sure they had a connection but only when you surrender your soul to the other completely does the star strand create a true bond of love. You have to choose it, just as it chooses you."

"Did the Fates take the Prince to get recycled too?"

"No, however unfortunately he was so heartbroken, not only by Malishca's betrayal but her loss. He slit his throat that same night in the temple of the Fates."

"Oof that's rough. Okay, so Malishca is recycled into Brigitta. Vamp Prince dude into you; also, what is his name, cause I don't think it's gonna work for me to keep calling him '*Vamp Prince dude*'."

"I believe his name was Asmund, Asmund Erebos Doyle Baldovino," I say pointing to the name on the family tree. "He was my great-grandfather's brother and the original bearer of my soul. However, Asmund's soul was supposed to be Thaddeus. My Father, Vladis Haben Markos Baldovino, told me this the night Briggita and I had come of age to begin our journey to unite and bond the clans for the following generations." I take a breath and gaze at the painting on the wall, thinking back to all those years ago. Memories that now seemed foggy but still poignant. Briggita feels like a distant memory with Jezebel by my side, I turn to see Jezebel staring up at me, and I reach out to caress the side of her face. She nuzzles my hand affectionately and smiles, then I continue.

"He told me the truth about who Thaddeus was, born of a rogue witch and abandoned at the castle when he was just a baby. My father knew that he was his first-born male heir. So, he took him in and raised him as his own. Hoping that he would have the other half of the *Steorra Erastés* soul. However, when Father discovered Thad's ability of magic, he knew that he would not complete the cycle. More than that it meant that he was a hybrid, half-vampire, and half-witch, thankfully his vampire abilities lay dormant."

"But he has fangs?" Jezebel questions.

"Yes, I suspect they are not real. It's all for show."

"Well, that's a tad, or should I say *'Thad'*, pathetic," she jokes with a laugh as she mocks Thaddeus.

"He has most of the physical aspects of vampirism, but never any fangs. At least when I knew him. I also noticed during that whole scene in the garden, that they were not there."

"So, you are telling me he wears fake fangs. For what possible reason?"

"I'm guessing for intimidation; he did grow up surrounded by vampires. Not being one himself probably affected him."

"Well anyway, I have to admit I am relieved to know he will not be sucking me dry anytime soon, no offense.

Please Sebastian continue." I stop and inhale deeply, I reflect on my previous actions. Retracing my steps to recapture the thread of my thoughts and find my way back to where I left off.

"My Father's theory for why he didn't have the right soul was because his body wouldn't be able to harness the soul of the *Steorra Erastés*. It would literally tear him in half and break the cycle forever. Father decided to dispose of Thad, since he no longer served a purpose, saying he was an abomination. He also feared for his own life, should anyone have discovered my father's infidelity. When it came time to complete the deed and kill Thaddeus, Father realized he had grown fond of him. So, instead, he raised him as his ward. Even still it was my father's responsibility to complete the cycle. He and my mother, Pavitra Trishna Baldovino, kept trying until I was born, the only male heir and future King. I think my father hoped that the fates would have pity on him and grant me the soul of the *Steorra Erastés* and reunite the clans."

"Wow, that's complicated, I can't believe he is your brother. So why is he so upset if he doesn't know he's your brother?"

"I would speculate he is simply jealous; we were raised as brothers. However, being the true Prince of the Sapphire Clan, I was betrothed to the girl he was in love with."

"Wait he was in love?" she asks, amused and almost shocked by this statement.

"Yeah," I say with a chuckle, "He was raised as a witch, or wizard is the proper term, so naturally he was groomed to find a mate amongst the witch clans. The closest being the Ruby Coven, and he didn't bet his heart on just any girl, he had to have *the* girl. The Princess of the Ruby Coven, Briggita Odessa Marta Sanballet, whom he would soon find out he could not pursue because she was the other half of the *Steorra Erastés*."

"So, what did Briggita do to get recycled?"

"She struggled to her duty as my other half, and to her heart. He did everything in his power to convince her to choose him instead. We all grew up together and I think if she didn't have to choose me, she wouldn't have. She and Thad were in love, however she felt it was her responsibility to the clans to complete the Merge. So, we were together, and I fell for her just as he had. Thaddeus didn't like this so in a rage and as an act of revenge he took her by force."

"Wait you mean he..." her voice tapering off not being able to say the words.

"Yes, he raped her," I say solemnly, haunted by the memory of that night. Finding it too much to bare I turn away, taking a moment to cope with the images suddenly stirring in my mind. Then once I collect myself, I turn back to face her, "I was there that night, the night he took her, thankfully I was able to stop him from before things went too far. But I was too late to do anything about him forcing himself onto her." I pause for a moment, once again finding it hard to have the courage to recall that fateful night.

"Later that night after she had recovered from the attack, I asked her to tell me what happened. She said that she confessed her love for Thad. He tried to convince her to leave with him, but she declined. Saying that if he truly loved her in return, he would understand that she had a job to do, and it meant they couldn't be together. He then asked her to lay with him just once and then he would leave her to her duty. She was in love with him and swept up in the moment, so she agreed. However, she changed her mind just moments before anything could happen between them." Pausing to catch my breath, I once more glance at the tapestry on the wall and continue.

"This angered Thaddeus, that she would go back on her word, so he took her by force. The fact that she even felt feelings for another and consented, despite the fact she changed her mind, tainted her soul. She was deemed an *Ainigma* and thus once more taken by the Fates come judgment day."

"Wow. It is crazy to think of someone doing these things. Then I remember that someone was basically me."

"Not really. Yes, you have the same soul, but you are still your own person and capable of making your own choices."

"That's a relief, I was terrified I would make the same mistakes."

"There is one more thing you need to know."

"Oh goddess, go ahead. I mean how much worse could things get at this point?"

"Even though I was able to intervene in Thad's violence against Briggita she did end up birthing his child nine months later."

"Holy crap!" she exclaims as if realizing something else.

"What is it?" I ask intrigued.

"This morning when I was getting ready to leave, I went into your room to get my phone, and I saw Briggita standing next to the bed. She was glowing like she a was hologram or something. It felt weird like I was seeing a ghost, it's kind of hard to explain, but today is the first time I ever experienced something like that."

"This is a good sign; it means your magic is getting stronger. I remember Briggita telling me of similar experiences. What else happened in this vision?"

"She was talking to Blink about being pregnant and not knowing how to tell you. Well, I guess that cats' out of the bag, pun intended." she pauses to have a quick laugh at her jest, then continues, "Then she went into the foyer and began writing in a journal. Then you came into the room, you talked and laughed, and then you both disappeared." She states focused as if seeing it happen all over again. "Do you know if we could find her journal? It would probably have a lot of useful information."

"We can try. I bet you are right, she was always chronically everything, I never thought much of it until now."

"I am guessing it was Thad's kid she was talking about in the vision. What happened to the baby?"

"Well, she had a little girl, her name was Makenzie Marta Durrell. She was born a month before Brigitta's soul was reaped and dragged to the spirit realm. I gave the baby to a neighboring witch coven, there was a couple who wanted a family of their own but could not conceive. I knew they would be able to raise her and teach her to use her magic responsibly. Unfortunately, this was also when the villagers began to retaliate and so began the witch trials."

"Oh no!" Jezebel whined knowing exactly where I was going with my story.

"Yeah, the witch covens fled into hiding and I never saw her again, I do not even know if she was able to make it past infancy."

"I'm so sorry Sebastian, that is horrible. Thank you for telling me all this, it answers a lot of my questions. It also brings up some new ones though."

"Well, I am done trying to protect you from the truth, I know now that you are strong enough to handle it. Besides, it is important for you to know all the facts. So please ask your questions."

"Okay, so I am just going to say them all at once. Try and keep up. First, did Briggita not love you at all? Does Thad know about his daughter? And why Durrell? Also, you said there were four reincarnations of my soul; Malishca, Brigitta, and me, who is the fourth? Finally, what is the Halo thing that Thad mentioned, or more like threatened me with?"

"Uh…whoa. I gotta say I am impressed with how well you followed along. That was a lot of information."

"Well, it's not like I didn't live it in some way so maybe I'm able to tap into the memories or something."

"Well, let's see here. No, I don't think Briggita ever truly loved me in return. She was only doing what she felt was her responsibility to her coven. I do not know if Thad knows about his daughter, he fled the castle into the woods the night he attacked Briggita and never came back. There was a third reincarnation of your soul, and her name was Antara Galene Sanballet. She was born in the year 1813, she lived for 129 years before she died in 1942. I don't know if you realize this but that was a long life for someone during that time."

"Did you love her too?"

"No, I never met her in person. I was still in mourning after losing Brigitta. My soul was created to bond with hers, and she never even loved me back. I mourned her for years, almost a whole century. Then in a fit of ravenous anger, I went on a rampage. It was the last time I ever drank human blood. As I have explained when we taste human blood *the frenzy* takes over and we become more beast than man, some more than others. Thinking back, I regret every second of it. During that time, I traveled from city to city enjoying the expansion of what is now the United States. Which is how I ended up here in California."

    She gazes up at me starry-eyed listening attentively, evidently taken by my grand tale. I suppose it is amazing and fortunate to be able to know someone who has lived all these years. Able to give you first-hand details of their experiences, feeling grateful she was indeed a stronger, more secure version of herself. This made me more confident so without holding back I refocus and continue my story.

    "Along my travels over the years, I stumbled into a brothel one night and saw a woman reading tarot for the tourist. A woman who looked exactly like the one I was mourning. I knew it was my duty to introduce myself to her and finish what Briggita and I could not do, but I refused. Knowing this woman may have the likeness of the woman I loved but was not her. That did not stop me from obsessing over her though. I even followed her here to California. I even attended her funeral after she had passed."

"So, why are you suddenly interested in me?" She asks very carefully, to ensure she did not misspeak the words.

Insinuating that because my love for Briggita prevented me from having feelings for Antara, she wasn't good enough to provoke true feelings from my cold vampiric heart either. Saying nothing at first, trying hard to find the right words and be able to say them aloud.

Terrified of the repercussions the wrong phrase may cause, knowing the truth would hurt her. I knew, however, that she deserved to hear my honest answer. I walk around the table and sit in the chair next to her, take both her hands in mine, look her in the eyes, and say, "Because sweet Jezebel, I am dying."

"What? How? Your Immortal!" She shouts as she starts to panic, tears immediately pool in her eyes at the news.

I chuckle at the morbid implications and irony of her statement. "I am only Half-Immortal, the other half lives in you and without the Merge Ceremony, I will die. This could not have been predicted. I did not realize how imperative the merging of souls was, in my selfishness, I forsake both our Clans."

"How long have you been dying?"

"Only for the last 70 years or so, after Antara died, I started to feel myself slowly changing. I am becoming more mortal every day. The years will soon catch up with me if I become full human and I will die. This is why I am so grateful to you; I did not know if I would live long enough to meet you. I also was not sure if my soul would return to this realm without yours here to guide it. It could have been the end of the Steorra Erastés, and the end of the clans."

"Oh, Sebastian! Well, how long do you have?" she inquires with a worried tone, tears now starting to flood down her cheeks.

"I am okay for now; it does not help I abandoned my true nature and no longer drink human blood."

"Would that help?" She asks eagerly.

"I cannot be sure, but the Halo Moon is only a couple of months away. I just need to hold on until then. Which brings me to the last question you asked, and I have yet to answer."

"Oh yeah. You sure you okay though, right?" she says wiping the tears from her cheeks.

"I will let you know if anything else changes."

"Okay, 'cause I meant what I said, I love you Sebastian and it would kill me to lose you. I was lost without you and that was before I knew you." She states lovingly stroking the side of my face softly with her hand as she says the words. Then she leans in and kisses me firmly.

I could feel the dampness of her cheeks as she pressed her face to mine. I did not care for I knew it meant she truly cares for me, and the tears are just another symbol of her affection. Then releasing the embrace, she looks deep into my eyes, as she so often does, just inches from my face and smiles.

"I have waited so long to finally hear those words, spoken aloud. I am so pleased that is you, Jezebel Jones, who is saying them."

"Really? Not just because I am the re-embodiment of Brigitta? Who you truly loved."

"Indeed. If I have learned anything in all my years, it is that unrequited love is the worst kind of love, and in some ways not even love at all. Love is something that is meant to be shared. Not feeling it reciprocated is barren and creates a void in your heart where the other should be. It makes my heart feel full to hear you clarify because I have had doubts." She says nothing, she just beams, and I see the honey glow in her cheeks flash bright pink.

Then I lean in and kiss her sweetly on the cheek, feeling the love emanating between us. Staring into each other's eyes, knowing that sometimes silence can say more than words ever could. It is obvious we are both feeling the fulfillment we have been longing for. Then both are alarmed and jolted out of our chairs as Jezebel's phone rang, interrupting our rendezvous. Then, after first apologizing to me for the disruption, she answers the phone.

"Hello." She says into the little box pressing it against her ear. I can hear the voice on the other end of the phone begin to speak.

"Hey, I am trying to find my way back to Sebastian's, but the GPS says his address doesn't exist." I hear Ashton say to Jezebel.

"Technically it doesn't," I tell Jezebel, "My house is merely an illusion, so you won't be able to find it using GPS."

"What does that even mean?" Jezebel asks me in confusion while holding her hand over the speaker so Ashton would not hear.

"Just give her directions from memory, you have been here enough times I'm sure you could act as the GPS."

"Okay, but you're explaining to me later what you mean about the 'illusion of your house'," Jezebel says to me before putting the phone back to her ear. "Okay, Ash where are you currently?"

"I just crossed the Golden Gate Bridge, 'cause I remember us going that way before, but now I'm lost so I pulled to the side of the highway." I hear the static voice say over the phone.

"Okay, Ash first I need you to give the phone to my mom so you can drive." Then she waits for the exchange on the other end and continues, "Hey Mama. Tell Ashton to continue for another couple miles on the highway until she reaches the exit to Wolfback Ridge road, across the overpass bridge and it should be on the right. I am sure she will be able to find it from there. I am in the middle of something, so I must go, and I'll see you soon." She says before abruptly hanging up the phone. "Okay we are running out of time, so quickly please tell me about the Halo Moon thing that Thad was talking about."

"Okay, it is called the Omnicentennial Halo Ritual. It is the merging ceremony that you and I will perform when the time comes. On May 26^{th,} the moon will rise in the sky aligned with Pollux and Castor, the heads of the Gemini constellation from which the strand of stars connecting our souls was taken." I answer while lying down on another wax tapestry. This one is a moon chart to mark the coming of the Omnicentennial Halo moon.

"Wait, May 26th, is my twenty-sixth birth..."

"Birthday. Remember, the Fates survey souls at the end of their twenty-fifth year."

"So, you mean I could be…recycled?"

"Unfortunately, yes," I say solemnly, disturbed by the mere thought of losing Jezebel.

"Oh," Jezebel said, clearly haunted by this information. "Okay, so how do we do the ritual thing?"

"When the moon rises in the air every 100 years on the anniversary of the first Steorra Erastés, it is marked with two intersecting halos around the moon. One red and one blue. During this time, the moon is perfectly in line with Pollux and Castor, the heads of the Gemini constellation. The strand of stars that makes up the arms is the strand the Fates took to weave our souls. Only during this time does the constellation ignite with the power of the Halo Moon which can be used to perform the Omnicentennial Halo Ritual and join the two covens. However, the Sapphire amulet needed to complete this ceremony is missing and has not been seen since Briggita got recycled. We will need to find it if we are to complete this task."

"Just out of curiosity, what happens if we don't do the moon ceremony thing?"

"Well to be bluntly honest, we die."

"Are you serious? Like dead, like real dead." Jezebel stammers in shock.

"Real dead." I respond, frankly, "I am already on my way there because I did not merge all those hundreds of years ago. Because our souls are bound, we are dependent on each other's life force to continue living. If am being honest, I have a sense that because your soul has been recycled so many times already, I doubt it will be granted another. Especially without mine here to guide it."

"So, why does Thad want me, if he already got her?" She said, pointing to the painting of Briggita that hung in the Sacred study.

"That I do not know. Which is why I am so protective of you. It can't be as simple as, 'because you look like her and he thinks you'll fall in love with him the way she did.' It has to be more complex than that, I just can't figure out what. Also, there is one more requirement of the Ritual."

"Uh-oh, I can tell it's a big one. Okay, what is it?"

"Because the halos around the moon cannot be seen in this realm, we will need to travel to Vasilia."

"Oh, is that all, just realm jumping." She bursts sarcastically "So, I suppose that is my job, right?"

"There is more than one way for us to enter Vasilia. One of them would be you learning the incantation for portal drawing."

Then just as I finish my statement Jasper knocks on the study door.

"Your guests have arrived Master Sebastian," he says, before bowing his head and making an exit out of the Altar Room.

"I guess we better go. I still need to get dressed." Jezebel says, seemingly overwhelmed by all the new information. I myself felt quite out of sorts with the interruption but am aware of the impromptus of the lesson while still having other plans. So, we depart toward the main part of the house. Passing through the doorway and making our way down the hall, the bookcase closing behind us sealing the magic away.

Chapter 8
Jezebel

W E WALK DOWN THE HALL AFTER A crash course in the history of what Sebastian calls the '*Steorra Erastés*'. Being part of the Star Lovers, I know it is my destiny to learn about the past and learn to use my magic responsibly. But that is becoming a difficult task to juggle with my job, and family always getting in the way. Not to mention the magnetizing pull I felt for Sebastian and wanting to spend every waking moment kissing and holding him in my arms.

After this weekend, my mother will be returning to Texas, and I will be able to focus on my Witchcraft. I just need to ensure her safety until then knowing Sebastian's psycho half-brother, Thaddeus, is out there probably planning another ambush.

"Jezebel," Sebastian says breaking my focus on my inner monologue.

"Yes?" I inquire, my brain pulsing from all the information.

"I know, this is much to take in, but it is important for you to know the history. I too find it a bit vexing at times, and I lived most of it."

"I understand, it can be overwhelming but mostly I just feel exhausted after learning so much."

"Well, nothing like a good dinner with friends and family to brighten your spirits." He says enthusiastically, after stopping at the doors to my room.

"Yes, I am excited but equally nervous." Then he says nothing, just kisses me on the cheek.

I open the door to my room and slip away inside so I can get changed into something more formal. I rush across the room and rummage through the closet for something to wear. Having found the perfect gown, I quickly throw my hair up into a messy, yet elegant bun and apply some light makeup. Slip into the dress and some cute heels, add some accessories and I am ready.

I open the door slowly, to see Sebastian suddenly so taken by my appearance. His eyes open wide and the honey glow in his pale cheeks beams bright red.

Wearing what could only be described as a floor-length purple goddess-style dress, with gold waistband accents and bell sleeves that drape down like sad wings. Accessorized with gold heels with straps that wrap around my calf three times and are tied behind my knee. Sparkling purple gems hung from my ears and around my neck, and of course, accompanied by the giant sapphire that always hung from my neck.

"Do I clean up nice?" I tease taking advantage of his bashful state.

"You look beautiful." He says swallowing hard, then holding out his hand for me. I take it feeling like a princess in a fairytale, as he escorts me toward the front of the manor. Then we walk to the great hall to greet Ashton and Mama at the front door.

"Sebastian?" I ask him breaking the silence as we walk, "I was wondering since the safest place for me is here in the manor. Would it be alright if Ashton and Mama stay until we can be sure Thad is no longer a threat? Mama is only here until the play this weekend anyway."

"Well, in all honestly this is your home too, and you are welcome to live here indefinitely and invite whoever you like to visit."

"Are you asking me to move in?" I ask my feet stopping abruptly, as I feel the butterflies tickle my stomach.

"Yes." He answers plainly, then in a nervous tone asks, "So what do you think? Or not? There is no rush, you can think about it and tell me la…" He yammers, avoiding eye contact momentarily unaware of me grinning excitedly.

"Yes! A million times yes! I would love to!" Then feeling awkward about my eagerness, I try to justify my answer. "I am here all the time anyway and I'd love to be near the Altar Room so I can practice my magic. So, yes! My answer is yes!" I shout enthusiastically, blushing while jumping into his arms and wrapping my arms around his neck. Thrilled by my answer he catches me and holds me up spinning me around, this only makes the fairytale feel even more real. My gown flowing before he places me back down gently, both of us glowing with delight.

"Perfect. Arrangements will be made for you to move in immediately. I will also have two rooms made up for your mother and Ashton for the weekend. The only thing I ask is no mortals…"

"In the Altar room, I figured," I say, interrupting him.

"No, I was gonna say my chambers, but now that you mention it, yes no mortals in the Altar room, either." He replies as we finally make it to the front part of the house and descend the staircase.

"Okay, your chambers and Altar room are off limits, gotcha," I say, making it clear I understood the ground rules. I see Mama and Aston entering the manor just as we cascade the stairs to the Great Hall. The Room is fully lit in all its glory, the crystal chandelier that hangs from the ceiling sparking. This makes me smile as Sebastian and I walk arm and arm together. We approach Mama and Ashton with welcoming smiles.

"Hey, Mama sorry I didn't see you this morning I had to run out quickly. Then I had work and came here right after, let just say it's been a busy day." I say as I greet her with a hug and a respectful kiss on the cheek.

Then as she releases me from her clenching grip she says, "That is alright Darlin', I understand. I knew when I planned on surprising you with a visit, that meant sharin' you with other folk. Had you known I was comin' you would have set aside some time to spend with me. Isn't that right sugar?" Mama says in her classic Georgian accent.

"Yes, of course, Mama." Then wasting no time, I grab Sebastian by the arm and pull him in close, "Mama, I'd like you to meet Sebastian Baldovino."

"Well, aren't you a stud," she declares as she looks at him up and down. Sebastian, being the gentleman he is, greets her politely by taking her hand and kissing it softly.

"Thank you very much and welcome to my home. It is a pleasure to meet the fine lady who raised this beautiful woman beside me. I look forward to getting to talk with you over the next couple of days." My mama, blushing bashfully in the presence of true chivalry, is speechless.

Indulge: Book Two

Then interrupting their little moment, I continue my introduction by saying, "Sebastian, this is my Mama, Lorraine."

"Lorraine what a lovely name. I am pleased to tell you that Jezebel and I have arranged for both of you to stay the night here. I apologize for the short notice but I'm sure we can accommodate any needs you may have. Starting with dinner which I'm sure Jasper has all but finished. Come, let us make our way to the dining room. Please ladies this way." Sebastian states guiding my mother by the hand toward the dining hall. Ashton and I walk side by side behind them whispering.

"Hey, is it safe to stay here?" Ashton ponders, "I know you spoke of some dangerous man before."

"That is exactly why you are staying here; the manor is the safest place for you. You will be under mine and Sebastian's protection, I promise."

"And you're sure Sebastian won't try to eat us?" she expresses, trying to sound as gracious as possible.

"Ashton!" I exclaim, a little offended by her comment on Sabbatian's behalf, but understanding of her concern. "No. He will not *eat you*. He doesn't drink human blood, hasn't for years."

"Oh, good. What about this other dangerous dude, is he a vampire too?" she asks as we enter the doors of the dining room to find Sebastian, pulling Mama's chair out for her and then sitting himself at the head of the table.

"No, I mean yes, it's a long story," I respond before breaking off and finding my chair at the dining table.

"What?" I hear Ashton say, clearly confused as I walk away. However, I know the explanation is too long to tell her, especially with my mother suddenly within earshot. So instead, I just ignore her and pretend like I didn't hear anything at all.

Indulge: Book Two

The long wooden table is set so beautifully with a white linen runner down the center. Each spot has a formal place setting with beautiful white dinner plates and silver cutlery. The servants take their time to pour each guest their water and wine, so Jasper can work some sleight of hand and pour Sebastian his drink. We all sit around the table waiting for our food and munch on the garlic bread sticks that are out on the table.

"So, Lorraine," Sebastian finally says, breaking the silence of the room that is filled only with the awkward crunching of breadsticks and sipping of wine. "Where are you from? Jezebel has told me before that she moved here from Texas, but your accent is far from Texan."

"Oh, I am amazed that you noticed, I am from Georgia. I grew up there and decided to go to Texas University after I graduated high school. Then I fell in love and the rest is history. We got married a year later and decided to settle down somewhere quiet and start our family.

Jezebel is my youngest actually, I have two sons who still live in Rockland. I do feel quite pleased with the life we have in Texas, but I do find myself missing some of the comforts of home. Like my mama's peachy pie, my mama could bake a pie like... Oh well, listen to me just rambling on doing all the talking. What about you Sebastian where are you from?" Mama asks Sebastian not even winded by her long babbling episode.

"Well, I am from the back east as well, but a bit further north. My parents came to this country from Italy and settled down in Pennsylvania. What seems like years ago..." Then Sebastian's story is cut off by the sound of Ashton choking on her breadstick.

"Don't mind me, I..." She tries to explain her sudden outburst but is unable. Instead, she coughs and wheezes trying to free her windpipe of the baked goods lodged in it. Startled by the event I immediately rise to my feet and begin patting her on the back until she can breathe once again.

Finally, I grab her glass of water and hand it to her, so she can clear her throat.

Once she is able, she begins her apology as we all return to our seats. "I am so sorry everyone, I was just so moved by Sebastian's story. Please. Please continue. How long ago was it?" she presses, turning the attention back to Sebastian at the head of the table.

"Are you sure you are alright Ms. Livingston?" He inquires politely.

"Yes, I am sure, please continue."

"As I was saying, my family moved to Pennsylvania many years ago, after they immigrated over from Italy. I took a cross-country trip to see all America has to offer. Before ending up here in San Francisco. Granted, I do have other estates across the country, but this has always been my favorite." Then he smiles at my mother and takes a drink of his wine-blood mocktail.

"Well, this house is gorgeous. What do you do for a living." My mother interrogates.

"I own a couple of Theatres here in the area. That is how I met your daughter; she attended a concert at one of the amphitheaters that I own."

"Oh, so do you guys work together?" My mother inquires naturally putting two and two together.

"Not exactly," he replies under his breath, playing it off with a fake cough, trying to hide something.

"What?" Ashton and I say in unison, equally shocked by the news but seemingly for different reasons.

"How long have you known that you own the theatre we work at?" I inquire trying not to make a big scene.

"Honestly, since the first time you introduced me to Ashton at the Chinese restaurant." He answers looking a little guilty for withholding this information from me, then continues, "I mean not immediately but I was doing some paper later that same week and had some forms to sign for the new play, and under the director's name it said *Ashton Livingston*, so naturally I figured the odds of it being a different Ashton Livingston was too far too coincidental."

"So, this entire time you have been our boss, and didn't say a word?" Ashton huffs, not trying her best to hide any part of how she is feeling. Then looks at me saying, "You didn't know about this, did you?' She exclaims, then just as she finishes, dinner comes out of the kitchen and is served gently to each person at the table.

We all glare gracelessly, politely waiting for the servants to finish before finishing our argument. The eeriness of the no one talking creates an awkward energy in the room. Then after they all return to the kitchen, I immediately pipe up, answering Ashton's question.

"No, I didn't," I say embarrassed to admit in front of my mother.

No one says anything else for the rest of the meal, we all finish our dinner in silence. The only sound in the dining room is the clanking of forks and the sipping of beverages. All the while the same eerie awkwardness hangs over the room like a dark cloud. Then as we finish our dessert my mother finally breaks the silence.

"My compliments to the chef, that was delicious," Mama says only receiving nods and groans in response. Still trying to relieve the tension my mom perks up again, "I think I will be off to bed then."

"I'll show you to your room Mama." I offer, getting up from the table, then taking her by the arm and escorting her out.

"Wait for me!" I hear Ashton call to us from the dining room as we make our exit into the hall.

We walk until I realize I have no idea where I am going. So, I stop abruptly, still holding on to Mama's arm. I try to figure out what to do but find it hard to focus because all I can think about is Sebastian's confession at dinner. We all stand frozen in the hallway until I hear a familiar voice.

"Excuse me, Miss? May I be of service?" The voice chimes in softly. I turn to my left to see Eliza standing there smiling.

"Uh, yes. Could you please escort my Mama and Ashton to their rooms?" I request, relieved to see her.

"Of course. Right this way madam." She replies holding her hand out to my Mama. Mama takes her hand and follows her. "I will be up soon to say goodnight," I call out, then turn and head back to the dining room.

Walking in the dining room to see Sebastian still sitting at the table, sipping his goblet. I pull a chair up next to him and take a deep breath. He does not budge, he just stares into the pool of blood in his goblet, watching it as he swirls it around.

"I don't even know why this is so upsetting to me, so I promise to let it go if you promise to stop withholding information." I start not even sure if he is listening, "I know I have responded in the past by running away or ignoring you. But knowing what I know now that must have really hurt you and I am so sorry."

Then he looks up from his goblet and grins at me, continuing I say, "But I am not that girl anymore, I am in this for life. So, you don't need to be afraid anymore. Tell me whatever you need to without fear of rejection. Please, and I will do my best to respond with the love you deserve. I do love you Sebastian and it's the craziest thing because we have only known each other for a short while."

"I love you too, and I know you doubt this because I have confessed how I felt towards Brigitta. I promise you this is different. What I feel for you is so much more than I ever felt for her. I will confirm this for you as many times as you need to hear it." Then placing the goblet on the table, he leans in closer and immediately meets my lips with a powerful, deep kiss. His hands press on my face lifting me from the chair until we are both on our feet. Standing pressed together I feel the warmth of his tongue slide gracefully between my lips.

Making my body tremble with desire, wrapping my arms around his waist, I pull him in even closer. Then in unison, we both pull our lips apart and hold our foreheads together. With our noses touching, we gaze into each other's eyes.

"Jezebel?" Sebastian questions softly.

"Yes?" I whisper back, as I pull my face away to see him more clearly.

"Would you please, stay in my chambers with me tonight?"

"I would love to." I say smiling ear-to-ear, "But first I promised Mama and Ashton a proper goodnight.

"Of course. Take your time you know where to find me." Then pulling away he walks around me, our arms reaching out toward each other until our fingertips could no longer reach.

Then he disappears into the hall beyond the doors of the dining room with a sudden gust. I chase after him, entering the hall to find no trace of him knowing he has sped off, somehow this only enticed me more. I hold my hand on my stomach as if to keep the butterflies from bursting out. Then I twirl around and rush down the hall the best I can in my heels and gown but couldn't help the rush I am feeling. I race upstairs feeling giddy and quite amorous.

Chapter 9
Jezebel

I ENTER MAMA'S ROOM TO SAY GOODNIGHT with a slight tapping at the door. She is wearing a new nightgown and is sitting in bed enjoying a steaming cup of tea and a book.

"Come in sweetheart." I hear her say as she looks up to me lurking in her doorway.

"Did you get everything you needed Mama?" I inquire.

Berlin DiVittore

"Oh Darlin', I don't know how you met this man, but please for my sake honey, you better marry him," she says with a perky smile, enjoying all the luxuries before her.

"Oh Mama, I guess that means you like him?"

"Like him?" She declares tuned in on my sarcasm, "If you don't marry him, I will." Then we both erupt with laughter.

"No, but seriously, Mama, tell me what you think?"

"Well, aside from the obvious money and comfort, this man has. He is a born leader, an awfully polite one at that. Such chivalry is lost on the generations of men today. And may I just say he is mighty good lookin'." I smile at my Mamas' opinions of Sebastian. Agreeing with everything she is saying, realizing I have never had such approval from her before.

Enjoying the feeling I say, "Thank you, Mama. I do feel deeply for him and look forward to our future together."

"And that means you're gonna marry him, right?" she says quickly, probing me for a verbal confirmation.

"Yes, Mama!" I respond with a giggle, "Happy now?"

"Why yes I am Darlin', thank you. He has proposed to you then?"

"Not exactly, but I don't doubt he will eventually. It's almost like it was written in the stars." I say, giggling at the truth in my words.

"You will let me know then. Anyhow, I ought to go to sleep now."

"Goodnight. I love you." I say smiling and kissing her cheek.

"Goodnight, Baby Girl." She replies before taking another sip of her tea and returning her attention to her book. Then as I start to leave the room, she speaks up again, "Jezebel, Darlin', I hope I didn't 'cause too much trouble with my question at dinner."

"No, you didn't." I start as I turn back to face her, "It was just shocking news to find out. Especially in front of you like that."

"I was also shocked to find out you didn't know what he did for a living." She says plainly.

"I knew he worked with theatres; I just didn't know it was our theatre. However, I'm sure Ashton is steaming right now."

"Well, you talk to your friend. I'm sure everything will be just fine."

"Goodnight Mama," I say again.

Leaving her on a good note I walk to Ashton's room, which is just next door. Opening the door and entering, I see her examining the room's contents, every little knick-knack and piece of furniture.

"I hope this won't affect your review?" I say mockingly. She gasps and turns to me, then flashes a snotty glare.

"No, in fact, I may never leave." Then softening her expression, she places the item back on the side table. "I see why you like him so much."

"No, even without all this, Sebastian is so charming to me."

"Yeah, sure." She taunts in disbelief.

"I'm serious. That's why I came here after talking with Mama. I need some advice."

"Oh really? Sure, I'll be your guru. Spill."

"Okay, but first I need to be sure you're cool about the whole *"him being our boss thing."*

"At first, I wasn't but now I think I am okay. Honestly, I was more mad thinking you were hiding it from me than the fact itself. But you said you didn't know so we are cool. Besides he's a better boss than that Bitchy-Office-Barbie."

"That is true," I agree, then we share a quick laugh.

"So, what advice can Guru Ash give you today?" She probes.

"So, after I went back and talked to him, we made up. I think he might have invited me to bed?"

"Yeah, and…you've slept in his bed before?" She asks confused.

"No, I mean for sex!" I state bluntly.

"Oh! You mean *to bed*! Well, again what's the problem you've had sex before."

"Yeah, just never with a vampire."

"Oh!" Ashton replies finally catching on to my issue, "Well I haven't either."

"I know but you're into kinkier stuff than I am. So, I'm guessing so is he, and I need to know how to prepare."

"Oh, well first change your clothes, as hot as you look in that gown and heels, you want something less complicated to take off. Don't worry about your hair or makeup, it's already very minimal. Be honest about what you are and are not comfortable with. I remember Michael was into some freaky shit and that was a problem for you. However, Sebastian's seems more open to your needs so I'm sure it will be fine." Holding on to every word she said, I took a deep breath.

"Okay, thanks."

"I'm excited for you and can't wait to hear every dirty detail in the morning."

I say nothing, just roll my eyes and smile coyly. Then after hugging her, I briskly head to my room to change my clothes.

I put on an emerald, green satin nightgown, with spaghetti straps and lace detailing on the back and along my breasts. I also slip into the matching bloomer shorts since the gown stops mid-thigh and peaks up in the back, exposing the bottom half of my butt. Lastly, I put on my slippers and made my way to his chambers.

I walk the short distance down the hall feeling nervous but exuberant. I have craved Sebastian from the moment I first saw his charming grin and dazzling eyes. I don't even think the fact that he is a vampire ever really mattered to me.

Knocking at the door, I hear his muffled voice say 'Enter' from the other side. So, I push it open, to see him lying on the floor in front of the fireplace. He is lying on a faux-fur blanket surrounded by pillows and there are rose petals encompassing the entire thing. Wearing only his black silk robe and some red pajama pants. The robe is open exposing his torso. The fire reflects off his buttery broad chest with a sexy orange glow. Closing the door behind me, I approach him slowly before sitting next to him in front of the fire.

"Good evening," he says in a husky, sensual voice. Causing me to involuntarily shiver as I felt his voice reverberate in my body.

"Good evening, Sebastian." Then there is a brief pause, "Well, this is nice." I state referencing to the blanket in front of the fire, as I stroke the soft faux-fur fabric underneath me, gazing into the ochre waves crackling in the firebox.

"Thank you. You look radiant this evening."

"Thank you," I say accepting his compliment, my skin warms, as if I am able to feel his gaze of adoration caressing my skin. His eyes gleaming as he cocks a sideways grin, I look at him feeling so safe and loved; something I had always yearned to feel. He moves in a bit closer until our gaze meets and I can see all the beautiful amber hues in his dazzling eyes.

I get so lost in his eyes, he looks at me and I get weak all over. I would submit myself to him anytime he asked, as long as I could look deep into his gorgeous eyes.

"Jezebel?" he says curiously. I hear him but I am so entranced I am unable to respond. Then he clears his throat to get my attention, I shake free of my daze.

"Sorry, I got caught up in your gorgeous eyes," I say without thinking, covering my mouth and blushing. He lets out a small chuckle and smiles at me, his eyes sparking. Grabbing my hand and lowering it from my mouth saying, "It is okay, honesty is good remember. I prefer honesty."

"You make me feel so…"

"Good!" He interjects, moving in a little bit closer.

"I was going to say comfortable." I correct.

"Is there really a difference." He teases in a voice that makes my body tingle all over. How does he do that I wonder. It had been about a month since I had met Sebastian and he had such an allure I couldn't resist, even after our rough beginning.

I seemed to find my way back to him, with almost no resistance. Here I am, sitting next to him on the floor, in front of a romantic fire. Something about its glow makes him even more attractive. Needing a moment, I look away from him and into the flames. Watching the fire dance and crackle, just a few feet from where we sit on the floor. Then turning back, I see Sebastian looking at me with a different kind of grin on his face.

"What?" I ask shyly. Instinctively I knew what the grin meant; I could feel its effect on my body. However, I needed to be sure before I did something I would regret, so I probed him anyway.

"You look amazing in this firelight." I blush having had a similar reaction to him, admiring his boldness to speak it aloud. "Would it be too much if I asked for a kiss?"

"No, it wouldn't be nearly enough," I respond not only to his question but to his boldness.

"Oh, well I will see what I can do." He responds confidently. As he rises to his knees, slowly and softly placing one hand on either side of my face, his fingertips barely caressing my hairline. The feeling of his vampiric hands on my warm, mortal skin made me shiver with delight. I close my eyes, as he guides me to my knees, and lifts my face to meet his. Seeing only darkness, I focus only on what I can feel.

His delicate lips press against mine; his kiss is soft but powerful. I feel the rush all over my body, it is thrilling as it electrifies my senses.

I reach out and place my hands on his hips, then his hand reciprocates accordingly. Moving one hand from my face to my lower back, pulling me in closer. Arching my body against his, I can feel how excited the kiss makes him, I moan with desire. Then I move my hands up his back pulling his chest closer, causing me to moan once more.

As the kiss grows deeper, our bodies grow closer, causing the desire to grow stronger. Then amid passion, Sebastian pulls his face away from mine and stares deeply into my eyes. His eyes roam as if he is looking for something deep within mine. Then they stop and he flashes a quick smile. He leans in once more, this time not for a kiss but to whisper softly into my ear.

"Jezebel, would you do me the honor of allowing me to pleasure your body on this fine night?" My body fills with his words, enticing me to the bone. Feeling him begin to nip at my neck with his lips, I had only one response. I squeal with blissfulness and utter the only thing I can manage.

"Yes!" With that single word spoken into the night, everything around us seemed to evaporate. He kisses my lips with such intensity it makes my head spin. Then rising to his feet, he sweeps me up in his arms and carries me to the bed chamber.

He lays me upon the bed, wasting no time, my hands began tracking his body upward to his collarbone, pushing his robe off his shoulders. The fabric glides down his arms and drops to the floor. Then I eagerly reach for the tie in his pants, only to suddenly feel my arms and hands thrown above my head as he lifts off my nightgown.

Not soon after I feel Sebastian fill his hands with my breasts, teasing my nipples with his thumbs. My back arching in sensual ecstasy. Then slipping off my bloomers and throwing them to the floor. My body shivers now being fully exposed to the night air. Then my skin finds comfort against his bare chest as we embrace for another quick kiss. My hands travel down to finish the job I had attempted before as I tug at the string on his pants.

Untying his pants and pushing them off exposing his perfectly erect penis. I feel a jolt deep within me begging for what I see.

Now both our bodies lay naked, our exposed skin shimmering in the moonbeams that spy on us through the nearby window. His hands trace my body as if memorizing every curve. Then his hands find my ankles, he lifts one and places it on his shoulder, and then brings the other to his lips.

He kisses me all the way up my leg until he reaches my thighs. Then he opens my legs exposing the source of my womanhood; a source I can see he craves.

He leans into my body kissing the inside of my thighs, nipping and grazing my skin with his teeth. I throw my arms over my head while letting out a gasp of excitement. My hands find the pillow above me and squeeze it as I feel him teasing me with his tongue. Then he begins kissing his way up my body, taking his time until he reaches my cleavage. He pauses, looks up at me, smiles, and says.

"Had enough?"

"Not even close!" He flashes a sexy smirk, his fangs seductively peeking out. Then he places his mouth on my nipple, softly kissing, followed by his tongue. Delicately licking and kissing my nipple while his other hand rubs my opposite breast. Then he switches. He groans with pleasure as if he is enjoying the act more than I.

I release the pillow in my grasp, my arms flowing down gracefully like the wilting petals of a rose. The pleasure stripping me of all the wasted years spent with past lovers. I place my hands on his biceps; his skin is soft, I run my hands up the back of his arms and comb my fingers deep in his long, dark hair. Enticing him, he snakes his body between my legs toward my face, kissing my lips generously.

"Are you ready?" he asks, his lips hanging off mine with every word. I answer affirmatively the best I can manage, the anticipation leaving me breathless.

Then he positions his penis with his hips, clearly to tease me a little and make me squirm. Without any more hesitation, he penetrates me, plunging into my body. I wrap my arms around him tightly and cry out in satisfaction. Feeling him thrust deep inside me until our bodies become one. Thrusting passionately, feeling the tension building until the sweet release. Then without warning, I feel something unexpected.

His fangs pierce into my neck, and he begins to suck, and it is the most ravenous climax I have ever felt. Then he looks at me with his honey eyes, his lips covered with liquid crimson, he slowly with one swipe licks them clean. Finally, his body tenses up and he cries out in satisfaction with one deep groan.

Removing his quivering member from my body he lays next to me. He smiles at me whilst I lay there, breathing heavily. I take one deep breath and exhale exhausted, never having felt so satisfied from someone loving my body.

"Wow!" I say, breaking the silence and smiling back.

"Yes." He responds, agreeing with my reaction. Then he kisses my cheek and grabs the blankets that are folded over the foot of the bed. He wraps both our naked bodies up in it, as we lay on the bed. I turn and curl up into the most comfortable spooning position I have ever experienced.

Berlin DiVittore

Feeling safe and satisfied I close my eyes, feeling his breath on my neck I feel him whisper, "Goodnight my Love."

Chapter 10
Sebastian

I LAY BARE WHILST ADMIRING HER SLEEPING naked body, I caress her skin with my fingertips. Brushing her long black hair back I caught a glimpse of the marking on her neck. The shame building inside me at the sight of it. I hate that I had just hurt her like that. In our very first moment of pleasure, the frenzy took over my senses and caused me to take advantage of my Jezebel; and feed on her. Even still just remembering the taste of her sweet nectar made me ravenous.

Then upon further inspection of her marking, I noticed something a little strange, Jezebel had only one bite mark on her neck wear she should have two. One from the rendezvous in the kitchen and another from just now. I tried to check the other side of her neck without rousing her sleeping body. Managing to see both sides I confirm there is, in fact, only one marking.

Feeling concerned, I quickly but quietly remove myself from the bed, dress myself, close the curtains, and head towards the Sacred Study.

I delve into book after book, trying to find any explanation for why a marking might have disappeared. Finding only information on the obvious answer, that they do not. I have been a vampire for my entire life, I knew this. Yet, I still need to find an explanation that does not confirm my worst fear and stir the pot. Knowing deep in my gut that whatever the explanation is, it is sure to *stir the pot*.

I then give into this feeling in my gut and search for another explanation for why a marking would not appear on a host. Finding only a few other alternatives but none fitting the current circumstances, except one. Body doubling, meaning someone else took Jezebel's form and posed as her to mess with me. Which is not only very creepy, especially if it was Thad, but also concerning.

There are only so many creatures in the world who can pull off full body shifting and only one of them can do it down to every strand of DNA, a succubus. Then I knew exactly who it was and felt incredibly moronic for not realizing it. I also knew this was going to be hard to explain to Jezebel. She is going to wonder how I did not realize it was not her, and after confirming our relationship it is gonna hurt more than ever. I start putting all the books away, going over in my head what I am going to say to Jezebel. Then before I know it, I can see dawn breaking through the curtains.

Leaving the Sacred Study, walking down the hall toward my office to make some final arrangements for the play. While sitting at my desk signing papers, I hear tapping on the door. My heart drops not yet being prepared to talk to her, I look up to find that it is only Jasper.

"It is only I, Little Bat." He says teasing me.

"Even after all these years old man, you still call me that."

"I was there the day you were born. I was there when your father forced you to feed for the first time, and every time after. I was even there when Miss Briggita left you devastated. You will always be my *Little Bat*." He replies, in an effort to make his point.

"I know. In many ways, you were more a father to me than the one I had." I say getting lost in my memories.

"Here you go," Jasper says, placing a fresh goblet on my desk, breaking my reminiscence.

"Thank you," I utter to him graciously, and then he bows and leaves the room. I grab the goblet and sit back in my chair continuing in the memories. Jasper has always been my faithful companion, accompanying me wherever I go. He was even there the day Thaddeus attacked Briggita. He stood in his way as he stole my horse from the stables. He even tried to convince me to introduce myself to Antara.

Then I take a sip of my goblet and hear another knock at my door, once again my heart drops, only to turn and find Ashton standing in my doorway.

"Hello. How can I help you?" I say, offering my services, only to be met with a look of disgust.

"Um, you have some blood," she states trying not to vomit, "on your mouth." Pointing to her face as an indication, grimacing in the process.

"Oh, I am terribly sorry." I apologize, picking up the fabric napkin Jasper left, and wiping my face.

"It's cool," Ashton responds, again clearly trying not to puke. Then entering the room, she sits at one of the chairs just opposite my desk. She continues, "I just wanted to stop by and clear the air about the whole *'you being our boss thing'* at dinner."

"Of course, I apologize you were blindsided like that, I really was not trying to keep it from you."

"Oh no, of course not. It's a massive coincidence actually, isn't it?" Ashton declares, almost in an accusatory tone.

"I do not think I know what you are trying to say?" I say confused, but firm.

"Oh, you just so happen to keep running into Jezebel. At the restaurant, and now you own the theater I have worked at for years. I don't think you running into her at the concert was as much of an accident as you claim it was." She says, starting to get steamed.

To avoid going into a full frenzy, I take a deep breath, finish my goblet, and address her civilly.

"Ashton, I will admit my presence at the Chinese restaurant was not fully an accident. However, I can assure you I knew nothing about Jezebel prior to the concert. If I did, do you think I would plan it that way on purpose?" I can see that I am breaking the foundation of her allegations, so I continue, "There are much better ways to meet someone than a lavatory door smashing my face."

"Fair point." She says, failing to hide her embarrassment.

"You will do just about anything to prove you are not afraid of me, won't you?" Just then Ashton turns beat red, avoiding direct eye contact. This time I knew I discovered the real motive for her visit. Speechless, she says nothing but glares at me as if to show she will not so easily give up. "It's okay, there are not many people who have stood up to me that way. Especially after finding out what I truly am. I respect that. It shows that you do truly care for Jezebel. However, I need you to understand something, I also deeply care for Jezebel. I promise you no harm will come to her while she is in my care."

"Easy for you to say now, but I remember what you did to her before." She finally states boldly.

"You are right, I did hurt her before, and I have regretted it ever since. Nothing about that night makes me feel good. I lost control of myself that night and I vowed to her that it would never happen again. I have vowed to protect her no matter what."

"Even if that means protecting her from yourself?" Ashton inquires.

"Yes. I would do anything if it meant she would be safe."

"I believe you, as hard as it is for me to admit, I can see that you really do care for her. In your own twisted-sicko kind of way, I know you love her. She is like my sister, so I wouldn't be doing my job if I didn't say something."

"I understand. I commend you for that, and I am happy to know that she is safe even when she is not in my care. I don't know any *'twisted-sicko'* who would dare challenge you." I say taunting her. She says nothing, just smirks and huffs in amusement. Then she reverts the subject back to its original course.

"Okay, but seriously. How do you happen to own the theatre where we work?"

"It was a recent purchase. The owner was going to sell it after your play was finished. When I was going through the offer paperwork, I saw your name listed on the current employee's list. So, it was actually you that swayed my decision to purchase, not Jezebel."

"Go figure." Ashton says surprised, "Well, I have some last-minute things to get done today. Please make sure that Jezebel does not leave?"

"Good to know we are on the same page."

"I only know as much as Jezebel is willing to share, and she isn't exactly very chatty about this second life of hers."

"She is probably just trying to keep you safe," I says, trying to reassure her.

"I know, but it kind of feels like we were doing life together. Then you come into the picture and now she is never around. She always seems to have some new crisis to deal with, which after the debacle in the parking garage, I have no grievances. The less of that I have to deal with, the better. I just miss my friend." After a moment of silent glances between us, she stands and leaves my office.

I take a deep breath and ponder the conversation in my head, I guess I never realized that Jezebel did have a whole other life she was living before I came into the picture. I never really considered just how much it changed and all she had lost and given up to do her duty as the 'Sanballet

Heir'. I check the time on the clock and wonder where Jezebel could be, so I ring my servant's bell for Jasper. He appears just as quickly as I call him.

"Yes, Master Sebastian?" He says upon entering the room.

"Jasper, do you know if Jezebel has awakened?"

"Yes, she is having breakfast with her mother and Miss Ashton as we speak."

"Thank you, Jasper. That will be all." He collects the empty goblet from my desk and makes his exit. I finish up my paperwork, which is mostly emails, and rush off to the dining room. I enter to find the ladies all laughing at something.

"What is so humorous?" I inquire.

"Oh, it's nothing really, Mama was just telling Ashton a story about my older Brother." Jezebel chimes.

"I am glad you are enjoying your visit," I say, taking my seat at the head of the table.

"Actually, I have to head out and do some last-minute things before the show tomorrow. Enjoy the rest of your day everyone." Ashton says before exiting the room.

"So, Mama, what would you like to do today? There is a beautiful garden here at the manor, or we can go out and sightsee or something." I hear Jezebel ask her mother.

"That's alright Darlin', we don't need to go anywhere special, I am fine staying in. Don't want to tire you out before your big day tomorrow." Lorraine responds, "However, I would love to see the gardens."

"Do you like botanicals?" I ask.

"Why yes. I do consider myself a bit of an Herbalist at times."

"Since when?" Jezebel interjects, weighing in on the topic.

"Well, I did have to give it up for some time, when my children were younger. But I am finding my way back to myself now that they are grown."

"I didn't realize that growing up, I apologize. I wish you would have shared it with me." Jezebel says comforting her mother.

"It's alright Darlin', it is a Mother's job to put her children first." Then nothing, just glowing cheeks and grateful smiles exchanged between the two of them. I watch them as they share a moment, happy to know Jezebel has such love in her life. It reminds me of my own Mother's love and kindness.

Then once again, I am taken back by my memories, remembering a time when I was a boy. Remembering my Mother's touch on my cheek and her melodious voice saying my name. I am taken back to that moment in time, and I can hear her as if she stands before me.

"Sebastian," The voice in my head echoes, "it is alright Sebastian. It is just your Father's nature to be fierce. He means well by it." She sat next to me on the stone steps where I cowered and brushed my hair from my eyes. Then I looked up at her, my face still covered with blood, and my eyes shimmering with tears.

    She opened her arms to me, and I climbed up onto her lap. She wrapped me up in a hug as I burrowed my face into her body. She began rocking me and humming as I sobbed into her chest. I listened to the beautiful sound of her voice as she began to sing, I could feel the terror of my father leave my mind as the sweet song of my mother's love and kindness filled my heart.

    "There now, there is my brave, handsome little prince." She said to me teasingly. I grinned from ear to ear wiping the tears from my eyes with my sleeve. "Now let's go get you cleaned up." My mother said as she placed my feet firmly on the floor and stood up. Then taking my tiny hand in hers she escorted me up the stairs and began to hum the same tune as we walked. The memory began to fade away, and her hum began to echo, replaced with the sound of another familiar voice.

"Sebastian." the voice called, I shook my attention free from my trance and focused on the voice. "Sebastian!" Jezebel says to me, I turn to face her, as my focus comes back to reality.

She was sitting in the chair just to my right, with both her hands on my hand and forearm that rests on the dining room table. My other hand is fiddling with the crescent moon necklace I always wore around my neck. Looking her in the eye, finally free from the entrapment of my own mind.

"Sorry, seems I was in a daze," I say apologetically. Then glancing around the room, I notice her mother has left. "Where is Ms. Lorraine?"

"Mama went to change so we can go outside. I'd invite you but you know…sunlight." She softly states, obviously a bit awkward for her to acknowledge.

"Ah yes, sunlight, the warden in my prison of darkness. I thank you for politely thinking of me anyway. Besides, you enjoy your visit. I have something else to do."

I say, still playing with the crescent moon hanging around my neck.

"I notice you always wear this. Why?" She questions as she softly plucks the charm from my grasp.

"My mother gifted this to me so I would not forget that it is I who is the Sapphire Prince and rightful heir. That I bare the soul of the Steorra Erastés." I explain as she looks over the silver charm.

"I often forget you're also a prince." She replies, delighting in my story, "The Sapphire Prince, how romantic sounding."

"You are royalty as well my Sweet. Remember you are the heir of the Sanballet coven, that makes you the Ruby Princess."

"Hmmm, well I always wanted to be a princess."

"Fate is humorous like that sometimes. Don't you think?" I joke tucking my necklace away inside my shirt. She responds only with a bright smile. "While I have your attention I am wondering if you are be able to meet me in the Alter Room later. We still have some things to finish up and discuss."

"Sure, Mama will probably take a nap later anyway."

"Until later then?"

"Later." Then she kisses me farewell, and hastily withdraws from the room. I then take my time walking to my bed chamber, for a little rest. It has never been strange for me to rest during the day before. However now I have someone to share it with, and I would do anything to be able to enjoy the sunlight with her.

Chapter 11
Jezebel

LEAVING SEBASTIAN IN THE DINING room and scamper off to find Mama. I discover her in the Parlour, examining the paintings on display.

"Mama, are you ready to go outside now?"

"Yes Darlin'. I was just admiring this fine piece of artistry. How beautiful the colors are and what not. Sebastian has good taste." She says trying her best to sound like an art expert, I find this humorous but brush it off as not to start something. Instead, I just politely pretend that my southern

Mama, who is more country than a chicken in a cornfield, can know a thing or two about art.

"Thanks, Mama, but I don't think he can take credit for it. It has been here longer than he has." I smile mischievously knowing just how long that was, trying my best not to giggle as if it were an inside joke or something.

Then depart the Parlour and head for the garden, arm in arm, together we walk, barely speaking as we walk through the house. She is still taken by all the amazing décor and artifacts. Finally, we approach the back door, I open it to reveal the beautiful bounty of greenery in the courtyard just behind the manor.

"Oh my." My Mama gushes at the breathtaking sight of the garden. "This is absolutely beautiful Darlin'."

"Isn't it, it has to be one of my favorite things about the manor." I state pleased by her reaction.

"Why on earth does he not open the house up to this wonderful view."

"He is just a little photosensitive, that's all." I respond proud of myself for telling a white lie with a half-truth.

We walk to the gazebo on the other side of the courtyard, threw the hedges that form the small labyrinth. The gravel of the pathway crunching beneath our feet with every step. I look around, suddenly getting flashes of nights spent in this maze. I see Sebastians red eyes staring into me as he clutches me tightly, and then flings me across the yard. I flinch at the memory, grabbing at my leg realizing it was only a few weeks ago and I still have the scars to prove it.

I try to focus on Mama, but the memories just kept coming, suddenly I see Thaddeus and his monstrous pet barricading us, my heart begins to race as if it were still happening. The hair on the back of my neck stands on end, when a memory of Sebastion and Thaddeus fighting on the rooftop overtakes my mind, followed quickly by the beast chasing Ashton and I in the parking garage. I can hear her screaming echoing in my head.

My chest begins to feel heavy, and my hand slips out of Mama's and before I can tell what was happening, I fall to the ground. Feeling dizzy and out of breath, I lay on the ground unsure of what to do, the world spinning, my Mama panicking at my sudden collapse. Still lost in the maze of memories pounding around in my head. The overwhelming rush feels like it is going to tear me apart, if the weight on my chest doesn't crush me first.

"Jezebel Sweetheart. Breathe!" I hear my Mama shouting, bringing my empty lungs to my attention. Then immediately I take a deep breath in, feeling my lungs expanding. Pushing aside all the fear and panic, I exhale promptly. Feeling relief as I regain focus on the present. I repeat this action many times, when I am feeling steady enough, I try to stand.

"Slowly Darlin'," Mama coaches.

Once on my feet, feeling her support from behind, we inch our way out of the sun and into the shade of the gazebo.

"Jezebel, are you alright Darlin'?" Mama inquires anxiously.

"Yes, I don't know what happened. I'm feeling much better though." I said, still feeling a little dizzy and jolted.

"Should we go back inside Darlin'?"

"No Mama, I am fine. Sit and relax with me." I say trying to forget the incident. Still hesitant, my mom sits next to me on the edge of the gazebo looking out on the beautiful garden. We sit in silence for what seems to be a long time. The only sounds are a few gardeners running a hedge trimmer and another a hose.

"Well now." Mama says huffing, "You did give me quite the fright Jezebel Darlin'."

"I'm sorry." I reply, still feeling dizzy and a sense of dread hanging over me. I do my best not to acknowledge it as not to spiral again.

"It's almost like that time when your brother Charlie was eleven and swept away by the neighbor's runaway horse." Then I smile knowing what she was referencing, and feeling relief from the distraction she unknowingly provided my mind. "Poor thing was so spooked by your brother hopping off that fence, it just took off. Taking your brother with him." Then we share a laugh at the nostalgia and connection of a shared memory.

"He still prefers to ride bareback." I say jumping in, "then he even taught Tanner how to do it too."

"That's right. Charlie was always such a pusher, but I guess Tanner was so timid he needed a push now and again." Then our laughs die down, but our smiles remain.

"Well, I'm feeling a bit run down Darlin'. Would you mind escorting me back to my room?"

"Not at all," I say as we both stand and commence our walk back through the hedge maze.

"You sure you're alright?" Mama ponders, checking in.

"Yes, much better," I say, now having a memory in the garden not followed by fear and danger.

Walking through the back door and up the stairs to the east wing of the house where Mama's room is located.

"Are you finding everything alright in your room Mama?"

"Oh, yes Darlin'. What an amazing treat, no offense but it is much better than that tiny apartment you live in."

"That is true. I suppose this is exceedingly better than a sofa bed." I say, cringing at the comparison of our rinky-dink apartment and Sebastian's luxurious mansion. Suddenly feeling silly for asking the question, even if it was polite to ask.

Then we enter her room, and I look around suddenly realizing that this was the room I was in when Sebastian carried me in from the courtyard. I begin to get flashes of memories again. I can see the IV stand next to the bed. I can feel the needle taking up residence under my skin.

I begin to rub and scratch my arm as if to remove the tiny invader from my flesh. Momentarily unaware that its presence is only a figment of my psyche. Continuing this action repetitively before feeling dizzy, and the heavy pressure returning to my chest. Then I see the grotesque scene I saw in my mind's eye when our hands touched.

I am standing in a dark space on a balcony, a set of stone steps to my right that leads down to the main floor. Leaning over the banister to see what is down in the room. It is Sebastian feeding on the frail corpse of a woman. On further inspection I recognize her, it is me, the lifeless body in his arms is me.

Shocked into a state of terror I let out a gasp and lose my footing. Tumbling backward but am caught by someone before landing on the ground.

"Jezebel! Are you alright?" I look up to see it is Sebastian who has caught me. He then helps me to return upright, and not soon after Mama rushes to my side.

"Maybe you should sit down Darlin'?" Mama suggests.

"No!" I exclaim forcefully, "I'm alright." Then looking at Sebastian I say, "My Mama needs a new room."

"No. Darlin' this one is," Mama begins before I cut her off.

"My Mama needs a new room, now!" I say it more assertively than before. Without any further questions, Sebastian rings the call bell and Jasper appears only moments later.

"Please arrange for Ms. Lorraine to have new sleeping quarters?" I hear him saying just beyond the doorway.

"Right away." Then a scullery maid helps Mama move her things to a different room. All while I stand frozen in space, everyone is moving around me in a blurred motion, avoiding eye contact. I feel pleased by my request being acknowledged but am still not able to shake the eerie feeling hanging over me.

Then instantaneously I remove myself from the room. The light is turned off and the door is shut. Jasper and the maid help Mama settle into her new room just down the hall in the west wing of the house. Then Sebastian approaches me.

"What is going on my Love?" He inquires, sounding concerned. Taking a brief moment to gather my thoughts, I take a breath and answer him.

"I am not sure, I am suddenly experiencing flashbacks, and it becomes hard to breathe, and I feel dizzy. Then everything gets blurry. I don't know what's happening to me."

"Sounds like PTSD," he states firmly but calmly.

"What? I thought that was something that only happened to soldiers?"

"No, anyone is susceptible. You have experienced a lot in a short amount of time. I unfortunately am to blame for some of it, I could never apologize enough for the pain and injury I have caused you."

"Thank you. Your remorse is enough for me to know you are truly sorry and regretful of the event. I suppose I do need to take some more time to myself to process everything."

"How can I help?"

"Well, I am going to make sure Mama is settling in and she will probably take her nap. I will meet you in the

Sacred Study and we will finish our talk. Then I think I will need some time in the Alter Room by myself."

"Anything for you." He says before giving me a peck on the cheek and walking away toward the Study.

I walk to Mama's new room; I tap on the door lightly and enter.

Mama is turning down the bed in preparation for her nap. She glances at me as I loiter in the doorway.

"Come in Darlin'." I hear her call to me in her melodious, hybrid Georgian-Texan accent. I enter and make my way to her bedside. She is sitting upright, with her book and reading glasses on.

"I don't want to bother you too much, but I need to reassure you that I am fine. After talking with Sebastian, he seems to think I am having some PTSD symptoms. It's nothing I can't handle."

"I trust you. If there is one thing I know about you, it's that you can handle anything. You have always been strong-willed and determined. That's why you didn't get much pushback from me when you up and decided to move away from home. I knew wherever you ended up you would be alright."

"Thank you. I didn't realize how much I needed to hear that." Then I give my Mama a big squeeze.

"I do hope you know, that if whatever you are going through becomes too much for you alone, to lean on the people who care about you for help."

"I will," I say smiling, fighting back some tears. Then as I am about to stand up, I feel her grab the Sapphire that dangles from my neck.

"Oh my! This is stunnin'!" She says dazzled by the gemstone as it sparkles in the light.

"Thank you. It was a gift from Sebastian." I say, blushing, remembering the profound words he spoke when presenting me with the amulet.

Indulge: Book Two

"You know my Great-Grandmother also had a sapphire necklace. She said it was a family heirloom, but I never saw it for myself.

"Then how do you know about it?"

"There was always talk about it, she was a very secretive woman. Anyway, it supposedly went missing after her demise."

"Demise?"

"Yes. Unfortunately, she was murdered. It was a real tragedy in our family. I only met her a handful of times before her passin'."

"How come I never knew this?"

"Like I said I only met her a few times, and it was hard for my Mama to talk about. So, I guess I just never did until now."

"Interesting," I say, more to myself under my breath than directly to her. Then I continue, "Well I am gonna go, Sebastian is waiting for me."

"Alright, I'll be here."

"Okay, sorry again about the drama, but this room is much better. I say as I look around the room pleased by the noticeable differences.

The setup is very similar to my room, but this room is larger. It has a four-post bed, with gold detailing and red velvet curtains. The furniture is all oak wood, stained a cherry red, with gold hardware and decorative paisleys. The day bed, just across from the large oak wardrobe, is upholstered with red velvet and has golden claw foot legs. The large rug on the floor has beautiful red, gold, and crème elements.

"It is a bit too much grandeur for my taste but if you say so." Mama comments, seeming still a little in the dark about the whole event. I know that I couldn't tell her the reason. I knew that the events from that night were best kept to myself.

So instead, I smile brightly, give her a hug and say, "Only the best for my Mama."

She reciprocates my squeeze before our mutual release. Then I make my exit from the room. Then hastily I rush toward the Alter Room, where Sebastian is waiting for me.

Chapter 12
Jezebel

APPROACHING THE BOOKCASE AND opening the entrance. Upon entering I notice Sebastian standing to my right, rummaging one of the bookshelves. I stand watching him momentarily as he begins to gather a stack of books in his arms.

"Need help finding anything?" I say, finally approaching him.

"No. Well, um…actually it would be most helpful if you could carry these to the study for me." He responds greeting me with a smile.

Smiling back at him I take the stack of books and carry them to the study. I place them on the table that stands in the center of the room. Then I huff, feeling mildly taxed by my efforts.

Then I turn and begin looking at the tapestry painting of Briggita. Without fail, my feelings of loathing encroach upon me. She just stands there smirking at me looking so regal and pretentious. The worst part is she does it with my own face. I know Sebastian has made many efforts to comfort me and rid my feelings of contempt. His efforts were not wasted, I did feel my jealousy has been relieved, for the most part. Somehow, I still feel irked by her, I furrow my brow and clench my jaw, feeling my emotions beginning to manifest physically.

Already feeling emotionally exhausted by the recent goings on I quickly approach the silk cord and close the curtain, hiding her snobbish face. Then I huff and grin proudly, feeling smug having bested my faux foe.

Sebastian enters carrying a few more books just as the curtain swishes closed. I turn and look at him, my demeanor changing instantly, feeling like I was caught doing something much more mortifying than closing a curtain. Granted it probably seemed more like I was fighting with the curtain or something.

"Everything alright?" He ponders slowly.

"Just peachy," I say grinning like an idiot, knowing he definitely saw me. Then we stare at each other awkwardly for a second, neither of us knowing quite what to say.

So, in an effort to remove the spotlight and refocus our mission, I say, "So, what's with all the books?"

"We ended our last lesson talking about the different ways for you to learn how to portal jump."

"Yes," I say confirmingly.

"So, the first option is you can draw a portal door with this." He says holding up a strange metal key. Intrigued I grab the key from him, finding it to be heavier than it looks. Continuing he says, "All you have to do is say *incantas intrare,* then the location of where you wish to travel." Then he hands me an old musty leather-bound book, open to the incantation page.

"Oh, that's all?" I say sarcastically, feeling the pressure. Then I place the key down and grab the book from him. Seeing the illustration of how to perform the incantation. I look at the text only to realize it is written in a language I do not know.

"Sebastian, I can't read this."

"Oh, right!" he exclaims, before hunting for something in the stack of books on the table. Then frantically he flips through some pages of a small but fat journal. "Say this," he says pointing to another incantation.

Nervous and unsure, I recite the words from the parchment as he holds the book open for me. "*Lingua scientia xéro omnia.*" Not a second after these words are spoken my head suddenly begins to throb, I grab my head with my hand. It felt like it was going to explode, and I needed to hold it together somehow. However, it only lasts a few minutes before dissipating.

"What the hell was that?" I question Sebastian demandingly.

"Look down." He says gesturing to the leather book still in my hands. Still confused but I trusted him, so I do as he instructed. Suddenly the words and symbols on the paper make sense to me. Stunned, my mouth involuntarily drops open, and my eyes begin to widen as they read the words on the page. I look at Sebastian amazed, and he smiles at me with amusement, clearly entertained by my reaction.

I look back at the book and instantaneously I feel my mouth begin to move as I read aloud in another language, that just seconds ago was foreign to me.

"That is incredible," I shout, tickled pink by my new ability. "How?"

"That incantation gives you the ability to read, write, and speak in any language."

"Well, if my Spanish teacher could see me now, I doubt she could still say I am a *fracaso sin esperanza.*"

"*Nunca podrías estar desesperado mi amor.*" Sebastian responds in Spanish. Turning me on like a light switch, I quiver and bite my lip timidly.

"I didn't know you could speak Spanish," I say, trying not to pounce on him where he stood.

"I speak many languages actually. *Faremo sesso piu tardi, bellissimo. Je vais me nourrir de toi aussi. Verstehen.*" Sebastian teased in various languages, as he slowly stepped toward me with a ravenous look in his eye. With my newfound ability, I understood him perfectly. This causes me to both tremble with delight and gasp at the words he so boldly spoke aloud.

"Sebastian!" I squeal, just as he steps into me entrapping me fiercely in his strong arms. I catch a slight glimpse of his fangs behind his seductive cocky grin.

"Should we get back to work?" I inquire meekly trying not to fall prey to his charm.

"I am only teasing." He states, releasing his hold on me and smiling.

"A little too well," I respond playfully. He says nothing, just gleams a final seductive grin, before turning back to the table of books.

"Anyway," Sebastian says refocusing on the task, undoubtedly as much for himself as for me. "To open a portal, you can use the *Porta Clavem,* or portal key, and the incantation, which you can now read. The second option is you can use this spell which will allow you to teleport to Vasileia." Then he opens up another book and sets it next to the others that I have just placed on the table. "The only issue with this option is I don't believe you have the magical strength to perform it. It takes a lot of *Magi Vi* to be able to teleport yourself, let alone take someone with you."

Indulge: Book Two

"Um, excuse you I am the Ruby Princess. I am a Sanballet. I will find the *Magi Vi.*" I say firmly looking at him haughtily.

"Well then, I look forward to you learning it. Best of luck. I knew many bloodborne witches who were unable to perform it as well." He says.

"Well, unfortunately for you I am the witch and the only one with magic. So, challenge accepted."

"With this option I do want to note that we are able to increase your Magi Vi, but it's risky."

"How?"

"Well, I know a witch up north and she will perform a blood ritual but like I said it's really risky."

"What would happen exactly?"

"Well, first off, the witch is not exactly very friendly, she's kind of a spinster. So, we would have to get her to agree first of all. If she does agree, you would take a bath in a special pool and lay on a Ritualistic Stone Table, commonly called a *Mensam*, and cut both your wrists. She will then collect your blood in a goblet, mix in a vial of your ancestor's blood, say an incantation and you will drink it. If you heal then your *Magi Vi* will be stronger, if not, you will die."

"So, lots of risk then. Put that at the bottom of the list."

"This is only if you don't manage to hone the power on your own. Traditionally you are meant to be taught by another witch. I only had brief lessons, and they weren't even mine. I may not be the best option for you to learn to master your skills."

"Well, what is the other option for opening a portal?"

"Well, I don't know if it will work anymore, but there is an old Cathedral that links Vasileia to this world. We would summon the fate Parasma, and she will open a portal allowing us to enter. However, there is a catch, this can only be performed one way. We may never be able to return to this realm."

Indulge: Book Two

"Wow, so there is the direct but hard method, the very hard and potentially deadly method, and the maybe not even possible but permanent method. However, will we decide?" I say being blunt and sarcastic. "Where even is this Vasileia?"

"Vasileia is the Realm from which all supernatural beings originate." he hands me an open scroll, with a huge, detailed map on it. I sit at the table and survey the map looking at all the different castles and villages. Then Sebastian comes and sits next to me at the table.

"This is home." He says pointing to a castle in the far-right corner of the map. "Sapphirus."

"Wow, so that is where you grew up?"

"Yes. This is where your family is from," pointing to his castle, he proceeds to slide his finger across the parchment just slightly to the left before stopping at a castle with the name, Arubis.

"Wow. So, we were neighbors."

"Yes, and this temple here is where the treaty was born."

"So how did you end up here?"

"Well, after Briggita died I fled Vasileia. Mostly to escape my father's tyranny who had begun to despise me, after I was no longer able to complete the bond. Granted I do not believe we were ever very close to begin with, but it only got worse. I also left to mourn the loss of Briggita and the betrayal of my once best friend, Thaddeus."

I have never heard Sebastian's story laid out all at once like that. I never realized what a depressing life he has lived, and to have done most of it alone. This made my heart ache for him. I stand up and wrap him in an empathetic hug.

"What is this?" He says, clearly caught off guard. Pulling away, I look at him and say, "I am so sorry that things have played out this way for you."

"It wasn't all bad. I always had Jasper; he is the one who basically raised me. Also, my darling Mother was always a pillar on which I could lean. However, I do appreciate your empathy."

"I always thought Jasper was just your butler-person, you mean he is a..."

"No, he is not a vampire, but he is immortal. When Jasper was just a boy he was cursed by a witch from this Kingdom, here," he paused briefly, pointing to the map. "She killed his whole family and put a curse on him so that he would have to live forever knowing that it was his fault they died."

"That is horrible!"

"Yes, he then made his way to the east until he reached Arubis. The King offered him asylum in exchange for his services and he had been there ever since. I always saw him around the other servants in the kitchen, being the closest neighboring kingdom, they shared their resources. Then when I got a bit older, I used to play by this river and he was there often, just sitting on the opposite bank. So, we just started talking one day and he has never left my side since. To the point where he followed me here."

"I am so glad to hear that you guys found solace in one another. I do feel bad for him though, what a terrible tragedy he had to go through at such a young age." I let out and involuntary yawn, "I apologize, I guess all this learning has made me sleepy."

"I understand. We mostly covered everything anyway. Now all you need to do is practice and come up with a plan."

"That reminds me, when I was talking with Mama earlier, she saw my necklace and said it reminded her of my Great-Great-Grandmothers necklace. Which went missing after she was murdered. Do you think it was the Crecent Amulet?"

"It is possible, but the last known person to have it was Briggita. I suppose it is a family heirloom, but I'm sure whichever one of your ancestors brought it to this realm did not share its history or even know its purpose. I do suppose it is worth looking into."

"Okay, I will ask Mama before she leaves in a couple of days. Also, I know we discussed locating Briggita's journals. Would they be in this other realm?"

"I believe they would, I didn't bring anything with me that I could not carry."

"So, you thought a big-fat-ugly book of spells was easier luggage."

"Let me rephrase that, I brought what I thought was important. I have gathered most of these books and supplies from this realm over the years." Sharing a mutual chuckle before moving on.

"Well, tomorrow is a big day, suppose you better get dinner and some rest."

"I will soon, I just want to practice these incantations a bit first."

"Alright, well I am off, the sun is setting, and I must venture out. Eliza will be here should you, or anyone else, need anything."

"Okay. See you later." I say, before he kisses my cheek and makes his exit.

I suddenly feel like a little kid being left home alone without their parents for the first time. I didn't quite know how to behave, and it was a bit awkward to be honest. Afraid to touch anything for fear "Daddy" might not like it. Then I hear Sebastians' voice in my head and the many times that he has stated that his home, is my home as well. I mean he did ask me to move in just yesterday.

So, I walk from the Study into the Alter Room, I look around to see the many shelves filled with countless books and magical trinkets.

"This is going to be fun," I say aloud to myself alone in the Alter Room. I wave while I watch him walking down the hall, until the bookcase slides closed, blocking my line of sight.

Chapter 13
Sebastian

L EAVING THE SACRED STUDY FEELING I have done my best to prepare Jezebel for what lies ahead. Still, I feel I need to do more to protect her considering that she is still quite a novice witch. However, I have been impressed with her abilities and her knack for learning things at such a rapid pace. Right now, however, I just feel like I have to catch my breath. My life has been changed overnight from the moment I met her, and while I am beyond pleased, I need time to process.

Making my way to the front of the house, having made preparations with Jasper earlier in the day to head out for the evening. He brings the car around just as I pass the threshold. We pull out of the driveway and before you know it, we are crossing the Golden Gate Bridge, and I feel the edge already beginning to subside. We head to this great little place downtown that I used to frequent a few weeks back. Being a regular and a VIP I did not need to wait in line, I just worked my way toward the door, gliding past the bouncer and his velvet rope.

I enter the club and instantly feel the vibrations from the music. I sit at my usual table and look out over the millions of mindless mortals as they let go of their inhibitions, by poisoning their souls with alcohol and grinding on strangers. The waitress walks up to my table for my drink order, and seeing as I was a regular, she gives quite the introduction.

"Well, if it isn't Mr. Dark-and-Handsome. Where you been the past few weeks?" she says in her usual squeaky East Coast accent.

"Good evening, Trixie. I have been preoccupied, but I needed a little relief." I say, trying my best not to flirt as I typically did. "I will have my usual."

"Alright, I see how it is, but okay one Bloody Mary coming right up." She says winky and then moving on. I felt weird not coming on to her, but also feel proud that my value of loyalty has not faded in my years alone. I am, however, still glad to have met Trixie, it had been nice to have someone know what I am and be okay with it. Not as much of a relief as it has been to have Jezebel know the truth, but nice just the same. The memories flash before me as if for the first time.

I stumbled into this club several years ago, finding myself feeling particularly starved. This was back when I used to feed on humans. I had not had someone to drink all night, and I began to feel my throat tighten and the urge to sink my teeth in taking hold of me. Trixie approached my table, and I could hear the blood as it rushed through her veins and her pounding heart. I listened to it closely until mine was in perfect sync.

I licked my lips as I felt the frenzy starting to overpower my humanity. This is a feeling I have loathed since the day I learned I need to drink the blood of others to survive. This reaction somehow does not stop it from taking hold of my mind. In fact, I feel in some way it actually makes it worse.

So, there she was standing in front of me, blood pumping, and all I could think was how selfish she was keeping it all to herself. That is until I caught something she said, something I found to be quite humorous.

"You okay sugar? You are looking a little pale." I said nothing, I just laughed like a maniac, but even this didn't scare her away from me.

She instead sat next to me, which unknowingly for her was a bad decision because I was more beast than man at that moment. Uncontrollably, I grabbed her, looked deep into her hazel eyes, and said, "Don't scream." As I attempted the *Imperium,* which allows me to control the minds of mortals. However, she did something that caught my attention even more than before, she didn't fall prey to my invasion of her mind. Instead, she grabbed me back and looked deep into my eyes, and sounding quite thrilled she asked, "Are you a Vampire?"

I was stunned, but I also began to panic. To which she responded, "It's okay. I'm not afraid. In fact, I'm a Biter."

I was astounded, the frenzy in me thought maybe she was giving her consent, but still I felt in need of more information. Truly her reaction to this entire exchange really caught me off guard and my curiosity seemed the only thing more powerful than my hunger.

I looked at her clearly still confused, so she then lifted her shirt to expose a tattoo on her ribcage just beneath her left breast. It was a symbol of a bat hanging upside down but upon closer inspection I saw that it was in fact fangs. Above the symbol was the letters 'B-I-T-E-R.' This only confused me more. She clearly was trying her best to bond with me, but all could do was stare, feeling lost in the exchange.

"A Biter, you know Believers in The Ethereal Realm. We believe in all supernatural beings, especially vamps, and believe we should encourage them out of the shadows."

"How did you know that I was a…"

"Oh, your fangs." She said pointing to her mouth as she lifted her upper lip exposing her mortal canines. Shocked, I covered my mouth and looked around to be sure no one else saw.

"You don't need to do that. I promise if anyone here sees they will probably think they just had one too many shots or something and will soon forget. Besides, they are amazing, you are the first real Vampire I have met."

"So, you are not afraid of me?"

"No, in fact, if you'd like a drink, I'd be more than happy to help." Then, wasting no time, she pulled the hair away from her neck and tilted her head. I tried to resist but the Frenzy took hold and before I knew it, I was sampling Cocktail à la Trixie. I pulled away before I was even done so I didn't lose control.

"That's all?" she said, sincerely bewildered and clearly dissatisfied.

"Yes, any more and I will lose myself to the hunger," I said still feeling the pull as she placed a cocktail napkin on her neck.

"Well, if you're ever hungry again you know where to find me." Then she handed me a card with the B.I.T.E.R. symbol on it, a number, and a location. "There are many members, and they would love to meet you and help with any *urges*."

"Thank you again. This is a one-time event; I'm trying to start sticking to the animal stuff." I said, beginning to regain control of my senses.

"Oh, so Mr. Dark-and-Handsome, is noble," she stated clearly surprised and maybe a little disappointed. I flashed her a smile, fangs and all, and she swooned and beamed brightly.

Just then I am brought back to reality when modern-day Trixie places my drink on the table.

"Freshly squeezed, just for my guy." She teases with a wink.

"Trix, I know we have enjoyed each other over the years, but I feel I should inform you that I have recently fallen for someone else."

"Ouch, now that hurt," she says before sitting down in the chair just opposite me. "So that's why I haven't seen you around much these days."

"My apologies, but she is my other half."

"I forgot how sensitive you are, the other Vamp who comes in here is kind of an ass."

"Other Vamp?" I say puzzled.

"Ya, he's not nearly as handsome but he comes around now and then. He has reddish hair, yellowy-eyes, and he never wears a shirt. Only some old leather trench coat. It's a little bizarre really, but he still has that Vampire charm I am such a sucker for, pardon the pun." Then she laughs on her behalf as I put the pieces of her description together.

It was Thaddeus, which met he not only knew there were mortals who believed but that he had awakened the Vampire side of his bloodline.

"Trix, you have to tell me. When was the last time you saw him?"

"Um, it was today actually, not too long ago." I immediately stand and begin to scan the club. When I feel a familiar sensation from the other side of the room. There on the opposite balcony is my enemy. We lock our eyes with a look that could mean one thing.

This means war.

Chapter 14
Jezebel

I WALK AROUND THE ALTER ROOM LOOKING at each shelf with precision. There are bottles of strange liquids, jars of herbs, candles, small wooden boxes filled to the brim with stones and crystals, and many other small totems. There are leather-bound books, some new, and some old. One shelf has nothing but old journals on it.

I trace my finger over the binding until I stop at one with the golden monogram 'SB' on it. Having a hunch of what it could be, but then I thought that it seemed too easy;

too convenient. Intrigued, I pull it from the shelf and begin to flip through the pages. I was exactly right; it is indeed Sebastian's journal. Open to a random page I begin to read.

September 4, 1703

Father is up to his despicable behavior again. So, I have been spending my time in the stables tending the horse. I do enjoy horses. They do not care if I am a prince. They do not care of my destiny. They only know if I am kind.

Why did I have to be born a monstrous beast? Why could I not be born just like everyone else?

I will make it my life's mission to be kind always. I will fight the frenzy. I am more than my hunger.

Sebastian B.

Berlin DiVittore

Once again, my heart to aches for Sebastian, I could not imagine living as long as he has, all alone. Then I flip through a few more pages and stop at a drawing. It is a sketch of Briggita, I smile having discovered something about him that feels raw and exciting. He was a secret artist; admiring the sketch a little longer and on the opposite page was another entry.

March 15, 1704
Today I felt something I had never before experienced. I looked at her in a way that was new. I have known my entire life she is to be my betrothed but until today I did not care. Today I looked at her soft green eyes and sparkling smile and felt my chest get warm. I wanted her to touch me. I wanted to feel her lips...

Then suddenly I slam the journal shut, not only is this an invasion of his privacy but I also think it best not to fill my head with things he said about *her*. So, I place the journal back on the shelf. Just as I do a small white business card falls out of it. It read the acronym B.I.T.E.R. on it, interested to know more, I slip the card into my pocket for later and continue my exploration. After making a complete round of the Alter Room I look up to the second level.

Again, I am still bewildered there are no stairs or anything to help get up there. Then suddenly I realize I know exactly how to get up there. I take a deep breath and crouch down slightly. Jumping into the air until I am flying. Feeling my weightless body untether from the ground I twirl around and glide upward, landing on the ledge.

Looking around at the new space, to my right I see a long table with dusty books and lantern scones hanging from the wall. Just next to the table is a large fireplace with dead plants on the mantle. Inside the firebox is a cauldron dangling above some old, charred timber. Then there is a large open space with markings on the gray cobblestone bricks that make up the floor.

Continuing to the right is a sitting area with a small armchair, a large sofa in the middle, and perfectly nestled under a window is a chaise lounge chair. Finally, front and center is a wooden coffee table. I approach the sitting area, to find the furniture covered in dust. Without hesitation, I lift my hand palm out, wave my hand, and speak aloud *'ventus'*, causing a strong wind to pick up blowing the dust clear from the furniture.

I turn and rush to the table and repeat this action. The dust clears from the table, the breeze causes the open book pages to flip. Then all the dust and cobwebs from the area began to spiral around in until they shot up and out of the fireplace. I look around admiring my handy work and start to feel at home. I grab the books off the table, approach the edge of the second tier and with a small leap of faith I step off gliding down to the first layer of the Alter Room. Then I place the books on the shelves where I suspect they belong.

I then gather the few Spell books Sebastian, and I had gathered previously, the *Porta Clavem,* and return to the second tier.

Holding the book open to the guide on how to draw a portal, I review it closely. Then placing down on the table I take up the *Porta Clavem* and approach the empty wall space between the windows. Following the instructions using the giant iron key, I draw a door shape on the wall. A glowing turquoise light sparks from the giant key as I mark the exposed brick on the wall. Then moving on to the next step I speak aloud the incantation, picking somewhere close as this is my first attempt.

"Incantas intrare Study," I say aloud.

Then the outline beams brightly, and a familiar door appears within the borders I have just drawn on the wall.

Still grasping the *Porta Clavem* I reach for the knob and turn it slowly. Opening the door, I am aghast by what I see on the other side, it actually worked. However, this wasn't the room I was trying to enter. Even still my curiosity wins me over and I step inside. The door closes behind me and disappears in a flash of bright light. I begin to look around, something about this room does seem familiar.

I look around to see if I can gather some context to figure out where I am. Tucked in the left corner of the room, just behind me is a closed door. Then a small seating area just to my right with a couple of bookshelves lining the wall on both sides of a small fireplace. The most prominent item in the room is the large desk that sits in the middle of the room, just across from the double-door entrance.

The wall is decorated with various pictures and antique items, mostly weapons. Moving toward the desk I see it is covered with papers, and a nameplate that reads, '**S. Baldovino.**' Then suddenly I realize my mistake. I said '*Study*', not '*Sacred Study*'. I am in Sebastian's office; granted it is a relief I am still in the manor and not trespassing on someone else's property; I still feel out of place. Just at that moment, I hear footsteps approaching. Quickly I run to the wall and conjure another door to return to the Alter Room. Just as I slip through the opening, I turn back to see Sebastian entering the room with Jasper in tow.

Our eyes meet briefly before the door closes and disappears once more with a bright flash. Just in time for me to catch the bewildered look on his face. As the door disappears on my end I fall back onto my ass. I look around to see I am once more in the Alter Room, on the lower level just next to the podium.

I smile feeling I have gotten the hang of this portal drawing thing. Feeling exuberant, I blast off the floor upward, swirling around the room grasping the *Porta Clavem* with both hands, as if to hug it. I celebrate with a victory lap around the room, zooming faster than I have ever flown before. Landing softly and perfectly on the second tier, I place the *Porta Clavem* down on the coffee table and flop backward onto the chaise lounge. Then I squeal with excitement. Whooping and hollering at the thrill I had coursing through my body before I am interrupted by a voice.

"Jezebel?" The voice calls out; I know exactly who it is.

"Sebastian!" I shout back with excitement; I look down into the Alter Room to see him looking around for me.

"Where in the devil are you?" He queries.

"Up here," I say standing on the ledge, he looks up at me with a wide grin. Then I step off the ledge and drift down to meet him exactly where he stands.

"Well, you've had an eventful evening."

"Why yes, I have! I can draw the portal, and I cleaned up the second level. I even flew some more, and I just feel so… so… alive!!!" I exclaim jumping up and wrapping my arms around him, my lips kissing him unapologetically. He lifts my legs, wraps them around his waist, and counters my kiss enthusiastically. Unexpectedly our celebratory, playful kiss becomes a seductive passionate exchange. Pulling away briefly looking deep into his eyes. He perks up a sideways grin, his eyes sparkling with amber hues. Still full of the adrenaline from my victory lap I take another leap of faith.

    Leaning in I whisper in his ear, "Sebastian take me to your bed chamber, please." Then I begin kissing his neck and nibbling his ear.

"Yes, my sweet." He groans. In no time at all we move swiftly through the manor in a blur and before I can focus on any one object we are in his room.

Chapter 15
Jezebel

STOPPING AT THE BED IN HIS ROOM I continue to kiss my vampire prince and before I can say anything else Sebastian throws me. Gliding through the air I am taken by the exuberating feeling, time seeming to slow momentarily as I feel the breeze and weightlessness of my body. Fall blissfully on the mattress just a few feet from where he stands. Thrilled by this I squeal, sitting upright I look at him smiling.

Standing at the end of the bed giving me a ravenous look as he proceeds to remove his clothing. Within seconds he is standing before me stark naked, exposing his vampiric cock causing my body to tremble. Only one thought going through my mind *'I need him now'*, my heart races in anticipation. Crawling on the bed, stalking his way up my body. Grabbing onto him as soon as he is within reach and embracing him with another passionate kiss.

"Make love to me Sebastian," I say breathlessly, continuing our embrace.

"I intend to my Love." He responds with a seductively husky tone. The sound reverberates my body, and I moan with pleasure.

Then he removes my garments and kisses my body. Finally stopping to toy with my breasts, his tongue and lips taking liberties with my nipples. I comb my fingers through his long dark locks. Completing his climb, he proceeds to kiss my neck, all the way to my lips. I kiss him fiercely; my tongue returning his liberties by entering his mouth. Startled when my tongue rubs against the sharpness of his fangs.

"Ouch," I exclaim, retreating.

"Sorry." He says pulling away, shame and anger quickly engulf his facial expression.

"It's okay," I say pulling him back toward me until he meets my gaze, "It is part of who you are, I just forgot briefly. I don't know if you know this, but you are the first vampire I have…"

"And I better be the last," he says flirtatiously cutting me off and continuing our kiss.

Wrapping my arms around him, my fingers slid up the soft buttery skin on his back. Then without warning, he enters me with a thrust of his hips. Thrilled by this I moan with ecstasy and call out his name.

"Sebastian!" This seems to thrill him because he lets out a deep groan. Our bodies collide until finally reaching their climax.

Then I see his eyes glowing red, and his fangs glistening from behind his lips. Getting excited for what comes next, I turn my head, and secretly ready myself. Then he penetrates me once more, only this time with his teeth. I quiver with pleasure as he begins to suck, only to be thwarted when he hastily pulls away, grunting and shouting to himself.

"No, I will not!" He exclaims angrily before quickly fleeing to the foyer of his bed chamber.

"Sebastian?" I call out with concern. Only to hear him grunting aloud to himself.

"No, I will not let you take her." I hear him yell in a hushed tone, as he leans against the wall, still naked. Quickly I put his robe on, which is lying on the chair in his bed chamber. Then I grab the throw blanket from the back of the sofa and toss it over him. Causing him to startle, he turns abruptly knocking me to the ground. Seeing what he has done, the red glow in his eyes dissipates.

"Jezebel!" he says in the normal register, his voice full of distress. He scoops me up from the ground and rushes me back to the bed.

"I am so profoundly sorry Jezebel. I have made a vow to never hurt you, and I have broken it on multiple occasions." He pleads apologetically stroking the bite marks on my neck, "I don't know how I could ever make this up to you."

Sitting on the edge of the bed, I pull him in close to me wrapping him in a hug. I take a deep breath and begin stroking the back of his head.

"You don't have to make up anything to me. Like I said it is part of who you are." I say comforting him, keeping the fact that I was starting to enjoy it to myself.

"I don't know how you have come to accept what I am in such a short period of time."

"It is easy because it's not *what* you are but *who*. I do hope that in time you are able to see yourself the way I do." Kissing his head and holding him a little longer.

Then pulling away, he looks at me with a slight smile, "Thank you my sweet, I do think in time, with you by my side, I will."

I say nothing, I just stroke the side of his face. Then he rises to his feet and begins looking around the room for something. Still wrapped in a throw blanket, he searches and scans the room.

"Sebastian, what are you looking for?" I ask, and without lifting his eyes away from his pursuit he replies, "My robe."

"You mean this robe," I say gesturing to the one I am wearing. He turns to look at me just as the robe slides off my body dropping to the floor, exposing my naked body.

"Yes, that is the one." He says dumbfounded and amused.

"Sorry, I had to borrow it, but I think I will be off to bed now." Then as sexy and confident as I can manage, I walk out of the room, completely naked.

Having made my dramatic exit from Sebastian's bedroom I race to my room before anyone could see me. Thankfully, the darkness of the hall cloaks me enough as I rush through the manor.

"Well, this adds a whole new meaning to the phrase *'walk of shame'*." Ashton teases, as she reaches the top of the stairs that are just across from my bedroom door.

Trying to play off my poorly planned wardrobe decision, I stand covering my bits with one hand and my breasts with my arm folded across my chest. I smile convincingly and say, "It was getting hot, so I took my clothes off."

"Good for you Jez, but that's not really what that song is about." She says making a reference with an amused expression. "However, I do have a sneaking suspicion that you were not alone in this decision."

Fighting the urge to laugh, I curl my lips in an attempt to resist the impulse to smile. Then folding my cards on the table I say with attitude, "Okay, fine. You are right! It is a walk of shame. Now come open the door."

Laughing, Ashton approaches me and turns the knob to my bedroom and pushes the door open. I rush inside swiftly covering my nudeness with the first thing I can find. Which just so happens to be my robe, thankfully. She follows me into the room, closing the door behind her.

"So, I take it this means you and your guy have been knocking boots."

"Yeah," I respond, normally I don't share much about personal details like this with anyone, even Ashton. But something about this seems different and I am dying to tell someone, especially Ashton, so without hesitation I explode. "Ashton, it is the best freaking sex I have ever had!"

Enthralled not only by my enthusiastic statement but also by my sudden willingness to share. She grabs my hands, pulls me toward the seating area in my room and we sit on the couch.

"Tell me everything!"

"Well, he is so sexy, I mean as attractive as he is, I did not expect it to amplify when he was naked, but his body is so amazing. And the things he does with his…well his."

"His dick!" Ashton blurts cutting me off, "It's not a bad word you can say it. Especially if you're having great sex."

"No, I mean yes his dick is great, but no I mean his fangs."

"Did not see that coming." She interjects, with a tone of concern and curiosity. "What do you mean? What kind of things?"

"Well, he kinda, bites me when he finishes." Then I lift my head and pull back my hair exposing my neck and the markings.

"Jezebel Jones, you kinky bitch!" She exclaims, genuinely surprised by my show-and-tell, "You *like* it when he does this?"

"I do. I am a little shocked as well, especially after I saw the real him so soon in our relationship. But I see a different side of him now. He is kind, humble and so protective. I feel so safe with him, I know he would never hurt me on purpose."

"Still, Jez this looks like it hurts, and not in the good way."

"I mean, it does but only for a second. Then he drinks from me and it's exhilarating!"

"And he does this while he cums?"

"Yeah."

"So, his dick is in you and so are his teeth?" She says, almost like she was trying to explain it to herself.

"Yes. I know it's a little bizarre, but I swear just thinking about it makes me want him again."

"Well, good for you girl. I never thought you were the type who would be into this but to each their own."

"I never used to be that kind of girl, but it is like he has freed me from myself. I was so trapped in my own head and now I feel so alive. So free."

"That is awesome. I wish I could fall for a guy like that."

"Really. I didn't think love was really your goal."

"Oh, thanks for saying I'm a *'two-bit-whore'*," She responds turning red.

"No," I say grabbing her hand and smiling, "I didn't mean it like that. I just never knew you were *the serious type*." I say imitating her and using her own phrase against her.

"I wasn't until I saw the way he looks at you. He *loves* you more than anything. He would literally die for you and be happy about it."

"I would do the same for him." Then there is a brief pause, and I continue, "I love everything about him, even the beast he thinks he is."

"Isn't he though?" She says clearly still on the fence about our relationship.

"No. He has more humanity in him than anyone I have ever known."

"Huh, maybe I should find me a vampire boyfriend." She declares mockingly but blushing.

"Maybe," I say not totally convinced, but still considering the option.

"Anyway, I should go to bed, big day tomorrow. Walk down to breakfast with me. I'm still not used to being here, while the luxury is nice, it's weird after reality sets in."

"Of course. Good night."

Then she gives me a brief hug and leaves the room. Feeling so ecstatic about this entire day I jump up and do a loopy loop in the air. Quickly regretting the decision after realizing I was still naked under my robe and catching the worst draft I have ever had. Shaking it off I slip into some pajamas and crawl into bed. Feeling so ready for whatever tomorrow brings.

Chapter 16
Jezebel

I WAKE UP FEELING ANXIOUS BUT EXCITED today is the day of the play and I am more than ready. This is my first performance since quitting my job and pursuing theatre. I am about to find out if I am any good and if it was worth it. I am also really excited that my Mama is here to see me perform.

In some way it made me feel like a kid again, like I had a school play or recital, and she is going to be there in the audience taking pictures with all the other helicopter parents. I get out of bed and rush to the bathroom to shower and get ready for the day. Standing in the shower going over the play in my head when suddenly I am not alone.

Sebastian enters the shower wrapping his arms around me and kissing my neck gently. Pleased by this intrusion I let out a soft moan, only enticing him further. He spins me around and pins me against the wall, kissing my neck with more ferocity than before. I definitely liked this but what really sends me reeling is when I suddenly felt him groping my boobs and caressing my nipples.

I let out a sensuous cry, already feeling so thrilled by our tryst I begin anticipating how much better it is going to get from here. This thought makes my loins tremble, and I begin to crave him.

"Sebastian!" I cry softly into his ear, just as he continues to kiss me wildly all over.

"Yes, my Sweet," he replies not losing his momentum.

"Bite me!" I squeal, feeling so aroused. This makes him stop abruptly; he pulls his face away but does not let go of our embrace.

"What?" He questions, noticeably caught off guard by my request. Placing my hand tenderly on his cheek, I smile. Still seeming a bit unsure by my request, he looks at me closely, as if examining me. His eyes rapidly scanning my face and neck, but all while remaining distant.

"It's okay. I want you to. I actually kind of like it when you bite me during sex." He looks at me hesitant and nervous, he starts to release his hold on me. So, I move in, quickly wrapping my arms around his lower back. Pressing his pelvis into mine, holding him as tightly as I could manage. Leaning in, I whisper provocatively in his ear, "It's kinky."

This makes him grin seductively, seemingly reassured, he begins licking his upper lip exposing his fangs. I slowly tilt my head to one side and close my eyes. He then cradles my head in his hand, the other on my lower back, and I fall weightless into his supernatural strength. Then his fangs penetrated my skin, I let out a whine of ecstasy as he sucks.

Then suddenly he pulls away all at once, groaning ravenously, his whole-body cringing, and his eye glowing red. He then hunches over against the shower wall with one hand up over his head, the other rubbing his mouth enticingly. I stand watching him with my hand over the open wound on my neck. I watch as his tongue slithers out entangling with his fingers trying to catch every drop of my cardinal red blood before it runs down his body washed away by the shower. I gaze at him like it was something I wasn't supposed to see. Getting off on the rebellious nature of my behavior.

"Sebastian." I tease, letting out my siren song. His eyes barely move to look at me but having his attention just the same I remove my hand from my neck and lightly smear blood across my lips. Looking at him temptingly I slowly lick my upper lip.

"You are a vixen, Jezebel Jones!" He grumbles as he approaches, wrapping me up and kissing me with ferocity once more. Then he lifts me, my legs straddling his body. His hands on my thighs as he holds me up, wasting no time he began thrusting. I grasp tightly to him as he rails me against the shower wall. The warm water flowing down our slippery carnal bodies.

Shrieking with pleasure as I begin to reach my climax feeling his member plunging deep into me. He reciprocates this action with a roar of gratification. Then he removes his vampiric rod from my lady temple, while still holding tightly to my waist. I then slide down his slippery body until my toes meet the shower floor.

We hold one another beaming with infatuation, out of breath I lean my head on his chest, sighing with a smile.

"Good morning." I chime casually as if our tryst is more of a habitual notion than a spontaneous impulse.

"Good morning to you my Beautiful Temptress." he mocks playfully before kissing my cheek.

I smile at him brightly, before turning around. His arms still entrapping me gracefully. We sway in the water as it rains down on us from above. There is a moment of silence. The only sound is the whispering hum of running water. Feeling relaxed in the cloak of steam gathering in the bathroom. We continue to sway when an abrupt loud voice enters the lavatory, imposing on our moment.

"Jezebel are you ready ye…" the voice begins before cutting off. I turn to see the blurring figure of Ashton through the foggy glass door.

"I am so sorry!" She pleads as she turns away, covering her eyes with her hand. "I guess we are even now." She says, clearly trying to diffuse the awkwardness with humor. "Okay, you finish up and I'll wait for you in the dining room."

Then she makes her exit from the room. Sebastian and I share a whimsical glance, matched with a cheeky grin.

"What does she mean you are even?" Sebastian inquires genuinely.

"Don't worry about it," I state, then proceed to cleanse myself briefly. Turning off the shower, I open the door step out, and wrap myself in a towel; Sebastian follows suit. I approach the sink and wipe the condensation from the mirror. I start to observe the piercings in my neck, mildly surprised there was little to no pain. Swiftly from behind Sebastian approaches kissing my marking.

"I'm sorry." he begins apologizing, a look of shame encroaching on his face.

"No! Stop!" I shout hindering his apology, "I asked for this. It was thrilling and received with nothing but acceptance. I am in love with you Sebastian Baldovino. Even the parts of you that you yourself find undesirable." Then kissing him abruptly but full of passion.

Next, he smirks at me bashfully before saying, "I have waited a long time for you, the love of my life."

"And I for you!" Saying with just as much compassion but trying hard not to belittle his gesture. His amber eyes flashed with adoration causing me to blush. Kissing him once more, but this time with sweet delicate lips.

"Never in all my years did I think that someone could ever make me see what I am, as anything other than monstrous. You are truly a marvel to me my Sweet."

"Not even…" I begin but feeling it inappropriate and embarrassing, I retreat.

However, Sebastian almost reading my mind responds. "No, not even her."

"How did you know I was talking about Brigitta?"

"You have often expressed insecurities about her in comparison to yourself. Namely in reference to my past with her." Sebastian states bluntly.

"Am I that obvious?" I ask coyly, being laid bare while wearing nothing but a towel. I quickly grab my claw-clip and make a break for the other room. Sebastian swiftly rushes passed me and blocks my path.

"No far, you have vamp speed."

"Plenty fair, soon you'll be able to teleport."

"I really have to make more time for magic lessons," I say tenaciously.

Then continuing the previous conversation he says, "I want to confess something," he pauses and sighs dramatically, "I know I said I loved Brigitta, but her love was unrequited. I now know what real love should feel like and see that I in fact did not truly love her. This only to say that you are the only woman who has ever truly had my heart."

"You did it again. Somehow you always know just what to say to me to make me feel better. Thank you."

"You are welcome." I smile at his kind loving words but then cringe at the following thought.

Quite noticeably because he prompts, "Say what is on your mind."

"So did you ever, you know, have sex with Brigitta."

"No." He states plainly, approaching me slowly and continuing. "We were never intimate. I merely stole a kiss or two. It was another time, with different views on relationships, specifically romantic ones."

"So were you a," I pause finding it hard to believe, thus hard to verbalize. "Virgin?"

Chuckling slightly before clearing his throat, "No, I was not a virgin. In my wallowing, I visited many brothels, and I am not proud to say it, but I have had many relations over the years." Having no words, I turn toward my wardrobe, put my hair up in my clip, and begin collecting my clothes. Then once more he says the right thing, "I now know intercourse is better with someone you love."

"No need to defend yourself. I am not upset; I was just trying not to call you a whore." Then he huffs surprised by my commentary, and I let out a brief laugh. "Okay now I really have to get ready, or Ashton is going to murder me."

"You are right, I will leave you to it. I also need to prepare for this evening." Then he gives me a peck on the cheek and bows politely, before exiting the room.

Finally, alone, I rush to get dressed and finish washing up for the day. Then running out the bedroom door toward the front of the house, crossing paths with Ashton on the stairs.

"Girl, we have to go, like now!" she says firmly.

"I know. I'm sorry." I shout without stopping.

"Eliza packed your breakfast. It's already in the car." Ashton says turning and continuing alongside me.

"Okay. I'm beginning to love that girl."

"Don't you think you've done enough of that today?" She jokes.

"Must you always torment me?"

"I couldn't help it; I was caught so off guard. But in the shower, good for you."

I ignore her as usual as we make our escape out the front door of the manor. We jump in the car and speed away.

I continue the ritual of running through the play in my head as I scarf down my breakfast.

"Work up quite the appetite today Darlin'?" My mother inquiries from the back seat. Ashton immediately bursts with laughter, at the implied innuendo. I smack her arm and begin shouting at her to shut up before exposing my extracurriculars to my mother. This only makes the situation even more amusing to her. My mother on the other hand looks quite perplexed.

Indulge: Book Two

I shake my head in mortification and gaze out the window for the rest of the ride. Instead, I reminisce about my new favorite activity with my Sapphire Prince.

Chapter 17
Jezebel

WE ARRIVE AT THE THEATRE BEFORE anyone else in the cast and Ashton and I separate. She went into the office, and I immediately went to hair and makeup. Linda was already waiting in the makeup room. She pulls out *'the book'* to reference my makeup and begins painting my face.

It felt like I was sitting for hours but was probably more like twenty minutes. Wasting no time, I rush to my dressing room and slip into my costume. Briefly, I review my lines one last time. I knew them all pretty well considering I'd been cast later in the play than anyone else. However, I was particularly nervous about the spells in the play, I didn't want to accidentally cast any magic and give myself away. I was playing a fairy, not a witch, and I had learned enough to know how to hold back. I left the dressing room to find the halls and backstage areas flooded with cast and crew. I walk to the stage and peek out of the curtain. The seats were already filling up with some early birds. One of them being my wonderful Mama. I smile at the nostalgia, if there is one thing my Mama hates it's being late.

It is nice to have the familiar face of my Mama here, suddenly realizing a void in my life that only she could fill. All this time I thought I had made peace with moving away from home. When in fact I had only locked my feelings away and thrown away the key. It is harder to forget something you have lost when it isn't around to remind you of how important it truly is to you. Having my Mama here suddenly unlocked the box, and my heart began flooding with emotion I thought had long ago passed.

    While I did not miss Texas, I did miss my Mama. I missed my whole family and the meaning they brought to my life. Having discovered my true self recently made the ache in my heart even more significant. *What good is finding yourself if you don't have family around to share it with?* And while I was finding a home in Sebastian, that didn't make my longing for my family easier, if anything it became more difficult.

    Suddenly I felt an ice-cold tear stream down my cheek, casually I turned away from Mama and quickly wipe it away with my finger. Then I take a deep breath and return to the present, stifling the resurrected feeling the best I could.

    As I turn around, I notice Ashton running around shouting at everyone. I quickly grab her, pulling her off to the side and away from her path of harassment.

    "Ashton, are you always like this before a show?"

"Like what?" She inquires.

"Scary!"

"What do you mean *scary*?" She says alarmed by my accusation.

"I mean you are yelling and sound kinda like a dictator or something."

"I'm the director, not a dictator. I'm merely directing."

"Well, do you have to *direct* so harshly?"

"I didn't realize I was. Do you think anyone else noticed?" she asks, seeming embarrassed and anxious.

"You just told Bethany you 'wanted a princess, not a drag queen.'"

"Jeesh, I said that?"

"Yeah, loudly."

"How many plays do you think I have been doing that?"

"My guess is all of them, unfortunately."

"I'm so glad you told me; I know I can be a bitch but damn. You know I'm really glad you're here. Not only are you saving my play by filling in for the Fairy, but you are my friend. I mean all these years, and no one told me to my face that I was being… well a dictator."

"I'll always be here for you." Then we smile at each other and embrace in a soft hug.

"Okay, enough of the kumbaya shit, we have work to do." Then she checks her watch and stomps off, wasting no time yelling again, this time at the lighting director.

'Well, you win some you lose some', I thought to myself as I walk away. I sit backstage in my dressing room waiting for the play to start.

One of the other girls I share the room with comes in, her hair and makeup are done but she is in her undergarments. She starts running around the room collecting the pieces of her costume.

She moves at a turtle's pace; I watch as she lays everything out ready for her to put on.

Then Ashton darts by before doubling back and poking her head in.

"For shits shake Jennifer, put your frock on or I'm gonna have to kick your teeth in." Then she pauses and looks at me, "It shit like that right?"

"Yeah." I mouth with a huge grin trying my hardest not to laugh, which only makes the urge harder to fight.

"Right." Then she pauses briefly clearly thinking deeply, then continues her train of thought, "We are on in thirty ladies, so final preparations." Then take off down the hall.

"Jeez," Jennifer sats, as she picks up the pace.

"Harsh but effective," I whispered aloud to myself.

"What?" Jennifer asks.

"Nothing," I say, trying to avert her attention from my comment. She brushes it off and finishes putting on her costume.

Before I know it, I am backstage waiting for my first live performance. I am so excited my stomach hurts; it is hard to believe how different my life was just a month ago. Now I have a good job, Ashton and I have never been closer, my Mama is here to see me perform, but most of all I have a guy I am crazy about, but even more so, he is crazy about me. I am living the life I always imagined for myself. *Honestly, now I'm just wondering how it could possibly go wrong.*

Chapter 18
Sebastian

I STAND IN MY BED CHAMBER, IN FRONT OF the mirror, straightening out my tie. The thought of Thad's daring grin burned into my mind. I try not to think about it as I get ready for the theatre, but it haunts me. He has so much power over me, and I know if I do not pull myself together, I am not going to be any help to Jezebel.

As of right now, it feels as if he is holding all the cards. I try my best to shake it off as I gulp my goblet, I can feel the blood coursing through my body bringing me life. However, I could also tell it didn't bring me my full strength.

I knew if I was going to be able to face Thad now with his vampire state active, I am going to have to drink the human stuff.

I look down at the half-empty goblet, swirling the crimson elixir around, I feel the reaction of self-loathing beginning to rise. I down the rest of the goblet and slam it down on the nightstand. Grabbing my blazer off the back of the sofa chair I speed to the front of the house, slowing just as I reach the front door. Then at a normal gait, I exit the manor and climb into the car that Jasper had running just out front.

I stroll into the theatre in a strut, feeling like a Rockefeller. I have been a man of means my entire life but something about the allure of modern-day San Fransico made it seem even more glamorous.

"Good evening Mr. Baldovino, right this way." The attendant immediately greets me and escorts me to the VIP gallery. I enter the gallery, peering over the balcony to the stage. Making sure I would have the perfect view of my beautiful Jezebel.

Then I turn and nod to the attendant, who is waiting nervously in the hall, signally my approval of the gallery. The attendant responds with a nod, closes the curtains, and then returns to the front of the house. I hang my coat on one of the wall hooks just next to the entrance.

I sit in the padded armchair and watch as the audience fills with spectators. It does not take much for the house to fill with people. The lights dim and Ashton walks out on the stage with a microphone in hand, encompassed by a spotlight.

"Ladies and Gentlemen, good evening and welcome to our show. I am the Director Ashton Livingston, really quick I just want to say a little thank you to our wonderful benefactor, Mr. Sebastian Baldovino." She says gesturing to my gallery, followed by a spotlight. I give a slight wave, acknowledging her gratitude and the audience's attention.

The audience applauds briefly and then fades. The spotlight returned to Ashton, "Thank you all for coming. Enjoy the show."

The spotlight disappears and she exits the stage. The orchestra commences to play, and the curtain begins to rise. Then character after character enters the stage a gives a brilliant performance. But the only one I cared about was my beautiful Jezebel.

Then suddenly I see her, she walks onto the stage and begins to speak, and I hang onto every word she speaks. Her voice is melodious, and her costume is just provocative enough to toy with the imagination. Then suddenly I see her rise into the air. Stunned she would do magic in public, I rise to my feet, then upon further examination, I see it is in fact a harness.

Relieved, I sit back down. She leaves the stage a few times, but she is also playing the part of the main villain, so I see her many times. Enthralled by her performance every time she returns. I am even impressed that she is able to speak spells aloud without any fireworks.

So astonished by her performance I cannot help but give a standing ovation at the end of the play when the cast comes back out for their final bow. Then the final curtain closes, and the audience makes their exit from the theatre. Quickly, I myself leave the gallery after first retrieving my coat, I walk to the vestibule.

I look across the entry to see Jasper standing by the doors with the bouquet of white roses I requested. I exchange my coat for the flowers and walk backstage, running into Ashton on the way.

"Brilliant show director," I say.

"Thank you. Pleased to hear you like it. I guess this means we all still have jobs?" she says in her typical snarky tone.

"Indeed." I retort to her snobbish comment. Then I return to my path, knocking on the dressing room door to hear Jezebel on the other side say, "Just a moment."

Then the door opens, and she is still in full costume with a towelette in hand, wiping the makeup from her face.

"Awe, you brought me flowers. Hurry come in," she says stepping aside. Wasting no time, I duck into the dressing room. I lay the bouquet on the vanity and then turn to face her as she closes the door. We stood in silence for a moment before she pipes up.

"So, what did you think?"

"I thought you were brilliant."

"No, really? So, you like it?" She says bashfully.

"Indeed, I loved it. I am thoroughly impressed you were able to cast without magic, that shows great improvement and control."

"Thank you, honestly that might have been the hardest part. Aside from the whole memorizing lines last minute and being lifted in a hardness in this gaudy costume."

"Oh no, I love the costume. You look so…. I mean you are…"

"Yes?" she says smiling with a little giggle, amused by my inability to speak due to her stunning beauty. "Well, one might say you are speechless."

"That is because what I have to say can't be said with words." Then I approach her, lift her, and pin her against the back of the door. Holding tightly, I began to kiss her, and she reciprocates enthusiastically.

I kiss her lips like they are the finest dessert I have ever tasted. Working my way down her neck and to her breasts which are still barricaded in her tight black corset. It had been decades since I'd seen a woman in a corset, but I quickly remembered why I liked them. Her chest looked so perky and inviting that I wanted to bury my face into it indefinitely. I could also tell there was another part of me that craved her. I could already feel the frenzy taking hold of me.

I gently set her back on her feet, and look away, with my eyes closed, I take a deep breath. Trying to regain control of my faculties.

"My apologies I seem to have gotten swept up in the moment." I apologize, now feeling like myself once more.

"That's okay, I like when you're spontaneous and 'swept up.' But maybe we should just sit for a moment." Then she grabs my hand and guides me to the old chaise lounge in the dressing room.

"Thank you, I am feeling better," I say my gaze slowly drifting away from her eyes down to her perky breast, once more getting lost in her cleavage.

"Sebastian?"

"Yes, my sweet?"

"Are you okay?"

"Yes, I'm just hungry. Well not hungry, I just want you so bad."

"Well, I'm yours, so take me."

Thrilled by her inducement I grab her, pull her in tightly, and kiss her keenly. Then I gently lay her on her back, filling in the gap just next to her. Our lips seeming forever intertwined, I take my chance and reach my hand below her skirt and caress the skin of her inner thigh all the way up. Seemingly pleased by this new move she lets out a little moan.

"Remove your panties." She does so promptly and lays back down. "May I?" I whisper seductively but with nothing but loving intentions.

"Yes." Then I began tickling the wet delicate source of her womanhood with my fingers. She squirms and moans in hushed tones, as not to alert anyone beyond the dressing room of our secret rendezvous. I kiss her delicious delicate lips as I continued to touch her. It wasn't long before she finishes with explosive cries of pleasure.

"Oh, Sebastian!" she says out of breath.

"Do you approve?" I tease.

"Yes! My turn." Then swiftly she rises, pins me down, and ruffles with my pants exposing my firm member.

"May I?" She inquires in a sexy teasing tone, that makes my body crave her even more.

"Please, do your worst." I challenge back, as I watch her lick her lips seductively. Then she places my firm cock in her mouth, something I did not see coming. I am pleased not only by her bold surprise but also by the magnificent sensation that overtakes my body.

And even more promptly than she had, I finish with a deep groan, my body tensing at the undeniable euphoria. Then I take a deep breath as another familiar sensation overtakes my body. I sit up and turn away, covering my face in hopes that it will pass. Then I feel her hand pulling mine away from my face.

Then I see her turn her head to the side, "Please if you really need it, I'm more than willing."

"Not this time but thank you. I am most gracious and relieved you have been so accepting of what I am."

"Again, it is not *what* but *who*. This is who you are Sebastian, and I love you! Why don't you?" Triggered by her question, I take a deep breath. Then I brush her off and do my best to avoid the topic.

"Not here, please. Let's get back to celebrating you!" Then she gives a coy smile, shrugs, and sighs.

"You're right. Sorry. Let's go to the after-party. I am sure they are wondering where I have gone."

Then I stand up and button my pants, making myself presentable again. She does the same as she slips back into her panties and changes out of her provocative costume. She puts on some modern-day attire and hangs her costume on the rack just next to the vanity. We then proceed toward the exit; I open the door as she exits in front of me before she stops abruptly.

Then she turns to face me, places her hand on my cheek, gives me a peck on the other, and says. "You will answer my question later, right?"

"Of course," I say, not fully sure if I meant it but knew wholeheartedly that she deserved an honest answer.

Then she turns back, and we continue down the hall to the front entrance where the after-party is taking place.

"There you are?" Ashton says to Jezebel as she appears seemingly from nowhere. "Do you mind if I steal her away?" Ashton continues, looking me in the eye as if begging to play with one of my toys.

"Of course not, she's all yours." Then Jezebel smiles at me before hurrying away and mingling with the other cast members.

Indulge: Book Two

I find myself a chair and sit observing, having attended many a party in my time I decide to sit this one out. With Jezebel's question still rattling around in my head, my heart racing just thinking about it feeling triggered once more.

Then a familiar face approaches me with a grin.

"Well, howdy Darlin'." Ms. Lorraine says as she sits in the chair to my right.

"Good evening," I respond politely.

"I hate to be a burden, but I am just beyond my years of partyin', I guess. Would you mind if I took your car home, and you can go with the girls?"

"Not at all, please let me have my manservant bring the car around," I say as I motion to Jasper who has been standing just off to my left by the front entrance. He promptly approaches and escorts Ms. Lorraine outside.

I watch them make their exit as the car speeds away when I catch a glimpse of someone just outside the theatre peering in through the glass doors. I look closer recognizing his smug expression and yellow eyes. Startled I jump to my feet and scan the room for Jezebel, having located her dancing with Ashton I rush to her side.

I whisper in her ear the discovery that I have made. I notice a look of panic starting to engulf her expression before dissipating and being replaced by an expression that could only mean one thing; she has an idea. She grabs Ashton and my hand and pulls us away from the crowd. Hidden behind the festive chaos we make it to the hall leading backstage without being seen.

Even still I keep a steady eye on the doorway to be sure we are not being followed. We enter into her dressing room, and I lock the door eagerly awaiting what Jezebel has to say. Facing the door guarding the room should it come bursting open.

Feeling my heart pounding in my chest I begin to feel anxious, unsure if I am going to be able to face this foe. Then the insecurities from the beginning of the evening resurface. Suddenly my mouth starts to water, and my eyes begin to glow.

Every ounce of my body goes on the defense, activating the frenzy. Know full well that I am at my strongest when I have human blood in my system. I tilt my head and crane my neck like a junkie eager for their next hit. Trying hard to shake off, aware that the only blood available is the girl I love, and the girl she loves.

Chapter 19
Jezebel

I RUFFLE THROUGH MY DUFFLE BAG, AFTER leading Sebastian and Ashton away from the party. Aware that Thad could be hot on our trail, I dig ferociously through my bag of crap, then I pull out the only thing that seemed to matter. The *Porta Clavem*, I press the large iron key to my lips, greeting it with a kiss.

"What is going on? What is that? Whoa, what is up with Sebastian's face?" Ashton suddenly speaks up and starting to panic. I rush to her side, grab her hand, and look her deep in the eye.

"We will be fine. Just breathe." I tell her trying to calm her down. She then starts deep breathing through her nose and out through her mouth in a proper inhale-exhale fashion. I nod to signal she is doing a good job.

Then I rush to Sebastian, who is still facing the door, and show him the key. Suddenly his eyes return to normal, and he looks elated.

"You are brilliant Jezebel Jones!" Then he grabs my face and kisses me powerfully.

"Why? What is that thing?" Ashton inquires once more, clearly still feeling left out and confused. Taking no time to answer I go to the wall and open a portal to the manor.

"*Incantas intrare* Sacred Study." The door appears with a sparkling turquoise flash of light. I then open it to see the shelves and shelves of books and trinkets. I grab Ashton's hand, and we walk through with Sebastian in tow. Then the door evaporates with a flicker of magic shortly after.

I place the *Porta Clavem* down on the podium in the center ring. Then I turn to Sebastian and in exact unison, we take a deep breath of relief and embrace in a warm hug. Taking our time to hold each other dearly, having escaped and feeling secure in our surroundings.

"Um, excuse me love birds is anyone gonna tell me what the fuck is going on?" Ashton demands, undoubtedly sick of being the third wheel in this endeavor. "Where the hell are we?"

"Calm down, we are safe. We are back at Sebastian's manor. This is the Alter Room, where he has been teaching me magic."

"Safe from what?" Ashton questions, still terrified by the goings-on.

"Remember a while back when I asked you to stay here 'cause of some guy."

"Vaguely."

"Well, he was at the theater tonight and we had to get out of there before he tried something."

"Wait, you don't think he'd hurt anyone still over there?"

"No, that is why we had to leave, to protect everyone. Anyone he would be interested in is here."

Then my mind began to race, and I suddenly realized I had forgotten someone. My heart drops and I can't breathe. I start to feel immense pressure on my chest and suddenly I become dizzy. Losing my balance, I start to fall over. Thankfully, Sebastian is still standing next to me and catches me in his arms. Lowering me to the ground slowly as my legs still give way beneath me.

"Jezebel!" He and Ashton both howl with concern. However, the only thing on my mind was our missing guest, Mama.

Then just like I had done for her just moments ago Ashton instructs me through breathing exercises. Having regained my focus, I am able to utter just one thing.

"Where's Mama?" Then Sebastian smiles with relief, which instantaneously fills my heart with hope. I clung to every word he began to say.

"I requested Jasper to bring her home just before I spotted Thad. They should be arriving any minute." With this news my heartbeat becomes regular, and I can breathe once more.

"Oh good. We should go greet them in the foyer." I say with relief. Then they both helped me to my feet, and we exit through the bookcase entrance. I watch Ashton gawk as the opening closes behind us, sealing away its secrets.

"That is amazing! I never would have guessed there is a room back there!" She shouts in sheer amazement, then continues, "How do you open it?" Pleased I am able to empathize and share in her reaction, I cup my hand over her ear and whisper.

"There is a little switch in the back of the second shelf, right corner." I smile at her and then run to catch up with Sabastion.

Running up behind him looping my fingers with his, we hold hands the rest of the way. We enter the foyer and sit patiently. Eliza enters shortly, and after starting a small fire in the fireplace looks to Sebastian and says. "Will there be anything else Master Sebastian?"

"Yes, please. I am feeling quite famished," I watch Ashton's face turn pale and her eyes bug out just at the suggestion that he is hungry. Which honestly made me laugh a little. Sebastian continues, "I am sure these ladies would also like a beverage."

"Yes, right away." Then Eliza exits with a bow.

"How many servants do you have?" Ashton inquires, kind of rudely.

"Just a handful, aside from Jasper. There are three housekeepers and four gardeners who maintain the landscaping and tend to the exterior of the house. We also have a cook and suis chef who come in on occasion. Eliza mostly helps Jezebel, but she also helps out around the manor as needed. She also lives on the property."

"She does?" I inquire, cutting him off.

"Yes. She is like me."

"Wait you mean she is a… vampire?" Ashton says turning even paler than before.

"Yes. I met her several years ago, she had applied for a job at one of my theatres. I figured out her little secret when she desperately fought to only be scheduled for night hours. Unfortunately got into a pretty big dispute with my manager. Instead, I offered her a job here as well as lodging for protection." Sebastian explained candidly.

Then Eliza walks back into the room with a tray of drinks. Some peach iced tea, tall glasses, and one gothic-style goblet with a crimson liquid. Eliza bowed before making her final exit from the room.

"So, who is on the menu tonight?" Ashton says teasingly to Sebastian.

"Ashton!" I scold her, defending him.

"What? Can't I make jokes?" Then before I could respond Sebastion starts laughing. We both look at him bewildered by his response. He continues in amusement while Ashton and I share glances until we both slowly perk up into a smile and then suddenly join in on his laugh-fest. Infected by his contagious laughter even though we still had no idea why he was so amused.

"What is so funny?" Mama says as she enters the room. Then the energy of the room dies down and we all look at her like we were teenagers caught smoking in the bathroom or something.

"Well don't stop on my account." She teases, confused by our reactions and expressions. All of us seemed uneasy by the sudden shift in energy.

"Hey Mama, so glad you made it home safely."

"Thank you, Darlin.' I am curious how y'all made it here before me."

"You know how Ashton drives, she is a little bit of a road hog." I fibbed, trying to hide the truth.

"Hey!" Ashton whined, noticeably offended.

"True," Mama responds, completely skipping over Ashton's retort.

"Hey!" Ashton complained again, scowling, then she continues, "Well apparently, I'm the pin cushion tonight. So, if you'll excuse me, it's been a long day and I'm going to bed." We all offered our farewells with a goodnight. She rises to her feet and approaches me for a hug. I politely respond by standing to meet her embrace. Then upon her release, she turns to face Mama and says, "It was so nice to meet you, Ms. Jones. I hope I get to speak with you before you leave for the airport in the morning."

"You are leaving already?" I inquire, looking at Mama shocked by this sudden news. I turn to face Ashton who suddenly has an expression of guilt on her face.

"Well, that's my cue," Ashton says before making her final exit from the room.

"I'm going to head out too," Sebastian speaks up, "and finish my drink in privacy, so you and your mother can enjoy some time alone together." Then he stands and grabs his goblet from the tray. "Goodnight, Ms. Lorraine I probably won't be seeing you before your departure so safe travels and I thank you for your visit. I have enjoyed your company."

"Thank you so much for your hospitality. It has been a real pleasure getting to meet you as well. I can see why my Jezebel is so taken by you." My mother says promiscuously, not at all hiding her intent batting her eyes at him like a schoolgirl. He says nothing in return, he just smiles politely before kissing me goodbye and leaving the room.

I turn to face her, scooting closer to where she is sitting, I politely offer her a drink.

"Would you like some iced tea, Mama?" She ponders my query momentarily, then responds.

"Well, alright but just a small one Darlin'." I pour her a small glass of the peach tea that had been sitting undisturbed collecting condensation. Then I hand her the glass, and she sips it generously while I proceed to pour one for myself.

"So, Mama, what did you think of the play?"

"I thought it was nice, but not really my cup of tea." Then she takes a moment to laugh at her pun, "None of that fantasy stuff ever interested me like it does you. I did enjoy watching you. You looked so happy up there on that stage."

"Really?" I ask, feeling my heart glow from my mother's comment.

"Yes, as a matter of fact, I have never seen you so happy as I have the entirety of my visit. I'm so relieved that you have found a life that excites you. Even without all these nice things, having people who make you feel good is more than a mother could hope for her children."

"Thank you, Mama." Then I set my glass down on the coffee table and approach her chair. Leaning over her I wrap her in a hug, holding her tightly knowing that this may be the last time I ever see her. I drop to the floor not letting loose my hold on her even for a second, crouched on the floor next to her chair, I envelope every second of my mother's embrace.

Then I let her go as I feel the tears starting to well up in my eyes. Turning away, simultaneously wiping my face, and rising to my feet, slowly making my way back to my spot on the sofa. Then I take a big gulp of my iced tea, I glance at the fire still burning in the firebox.

"Goodness! Jezebel Darlin' what is on your neck?" Mama suddenly exclaims, clearly spotting Sebastian's markings on my neck.

"Oh, it's nothing. They are just um…hickies." Then I give her a guilty smile, covering my neck with my hand. Embarrassed not only by her discovering my markings but also because I didn't feel any more comfortable admitting they were hickies either.

"Jezebel I am surprised at you; I didn't know you got down like that." My mother retorts, making me feel even more uncomfortable.

"You know, Mama it has been a long day. How about I escort you to your room? Let you rest up before your big day of travel tomorrow." She flashes me a cheeky smile, amused by my embarrassment, but plays along.

"Alright. It's none of my business anyway. Besides, that man clearly loves more than his own life, so things are bound to get buck wild time and again."

"Okay, here we go," I say, rushing her out the door as if it would make our long journey across the manor any less awkward. Not able to hold back her amusement any longer she lets out a small laugh as she ascends the stairs. I follow behind her, feeling uneasy about the discussion and her comments regarding my sex life.

I didn't make it more than halfway before Eliza came up behind me. I jump out of my skin as I notice her slender body appearing out of the darkness.

"My sincerest apologies Miss Jones." She says, before giving me a moment to return to my body.

"That's alright. I'm so glad it's you." I say feeling more normal about her presents. "Did you need something?"

"Yes. Master requests your presence in the gazebo I will finish escorting Ms. Lorraine to bed."

"Okay. Thanks." Then I turned to Mama, "Mama I have to go find Sebastian. But goodnight and I love you. I will see you in the morning for breakfast." Then I give her a brief squeeze and a kiss on the cheek. Making a break from the awkward situation I hurry down the stairs and toward the back of the house. I find my way through the doors to the courtyard and then to the gazebo.

I approach the garden house to see Sebastian sitting on the left side of the steps, drinking his goblet, and writing in a black leather-bound book.

"What is that?" I ask as I approach him. He looks up and smiles at me, then closes his book, marking the page with his writing utensil.

"Oh, I like to journal from time to time, when things get out of control in here." He says plainly, but with a hint of shyness, pointing to his head.

"You mean there are times when you're not stressing out?" I tease, not realizing how harsh it is until it leaves my lips. I try to play it off as a joke by smiling and lightly punching him in the arm and sitting next to him.

He says nothing, just smiles meekly, and gives a not-so-convincing chuckle. He places his book and the goblet down on the floor of the gazebo to his left. Then he turns to me, grabs both my hands in his and sighs. I start to get a pit in my stomach concerned by his vibe, not used to him acting so calmly. Starting to second guess his calm mannerisms for forced serenity almost like he was trying to stay calm on purpose.

"Jezebel, I want to say that I have been thinking about everything you have said to me recently. I am undeniably in love with you. I thought I would have to work harder to earn your affection but hearing you say time and time again that you accept me for what I am means the world to me. You mean the world to me." I wanted to let out a sigh of relief, but my inner voice was whispering to me not to let my guard down yet, like a ghost from relationships past.

"I love you too." I finally say, filling in his silent pause. He continues to pause, the eeriness drilling into my head with every silent second that passes. Every second a word went unspoken. Half expecting the next words to come out of his mouth not to be as pleasant as the ones spoken thus far.

"I am done, being ashamed of what…" He pauses catching his miss spoken word, and corrects himself, "Who I am. I was born this way but have been carrying this baggage around for centuries. I finally have someone who looks at me as I am and loves me anyway. Thank you, Jezebel, thank you for loving me anyway." A soft grin appears on his face, followed by a tear streaming down his face. His amber eyes glistening as the tears pooled in his eyes.

I suddenly let go of the clench in my stomach, the pit all but dissipating. Whipping his tears with my hand, I cup his cheek in my palm.

"Honestly, at first, I was a little shaken by it but then I fell in love with who you are. No man has ever treated me as gently and kindly as you have." I start to say, then removing my hand from his face and turn toward the shrubbery in the courtyard I continue, "I feel like when you love someone you have to learn to love the parts of them that are less desirable because, without those parts, they wouldn't have the parts of them you do love."

"So, you do find my vampirism appalling?" He asks trying to clarify my statement.

"I did at first but now that I have really gotten to know you and see it from a different point of view, I actually really love it," I say turning back to face him.

"Really?" He clarifies once more, but this time with a little more enthusasm in his voice.

"Yeah, especially when, well when," I struggle to get the words out never having said anything like this before. "Especially when we have sex," I speak coyly just below my normal register, physically cringing at the sound of them.

"Oh really?" He teases in a sexy, cool-guy tone of voice, making eyes at me with his eyebrows and flashing his usual cocky sideways grin.

"Yes, I find myself craving you," having already let the cat out of the bag. I just dove right in and let it all go, "and not just with your body but with your fangs. I love the feeling I get when you drink from me. Sometimes while you're still in me, I have never cum like you have made me cum." Then I put my hand over my mouth before any more words could escape it.

"Well then," He says speechless for a brief moment, "I love feeding from you, but I do fear I will lose myself and hurt you. The frenzy is not really something I can control."

"I trust you," I state endearingly looking him lovingly in the eye.

"Thank you. But I feel you misunderstand. It is not me but a symptom of Vampirism itself."

"I feel you misunderstand; it is like you said you are only half Vampire, the other half of you lives in me." Then his face lights up as if a spark was struck by this realization. Then I continue, "You haven't hurt me so far, and you have been able to stop yourself every time. Have you ever been able to stop before?"

"Not without great difficulty. I myself have begun to find it a bit peculiar. However, I've also never have never made love before."

"Never?"

"No, the only other person who I have given my heart to was Briggita and we were never intimate. Every time I have had sex was just to get off and I usually lost control if the frenzy took over."

"So, my guess is your mind or soul, or whatever recognizes me as its other half and won't let you hurt me. I guess it also helps that you love me." Then I pause briefly trying to piece together my next thought and continue. "I do wonder, you have never fed from me when we are not being intimate. If the same thing happens then I doubt making love has anything to do with it. However good to know you were a murdering-whore before you met me. So glad I could save you from yourself." I tease trying to justify his confession of killing the woman he had sex with in the past, with a joke.

"Me too." He responds, then kisses my cheek "I do want it noted that again, the only sex I have ever had was during a period of great mourning. I was lost." Then he gets close to me, continuing, "I feel complete being with you."

"Isn't it the girl who normally says cliché shit like that?"

"Well, I'm from another time, when the constraints of gender were not so finite," he explains plainly.

"Yes. Must have been nice."

"Well, it was a little chaotic if I'm being honest."

"I'm used to playing it safe and need a little bit of that in my life," I say smiling at him, dreaming of a kiss as I look at his juicy lips. Getting so wrapped up that I am surprised by what he says next.

"And I needed a little piece of serenity." He says clearly referring to me. I blush, still starving for a kiss.

"Come it is probably time we went to bed," He states raising to feet and offering me his hand. I take it and we stroll arm in arm in the direction of the manor. I feel so loved and suddenly I feel something I have never before felt. I feel that I would perish without Sebastian by my side. That is if anyone were to try and harm him, I would be lost. It was at this moment I knew I had to find a way to get rid of Thad.

He was a threat to Sebastian, and I must find a way to keep him safe. Even at the cost of my life.

Chapter 20
Thaddeus

STANDING AT THE EDGE OF THE NIGHT I watch them walking through the garden. I move in line with them camouflaged by the shadows. Feeling the envy building inside clenching in my gut so as not to get the jump on them right here and now. I peer at them, grimacing at them laughing like they didn't have a care in the world.

I bet they would feel differently if they knew I was here watching. I am always in the darkness watching them.

Observing their every action, preparing to strike at just the right moment.

Watching as they enter the manor, once they are beyond the threshold I step out of the darkness and into the light. Swiftly I approach the manor, and stare in through the glass, watching their silhouettes become more distant as they continue to walk.

I laugh aloud to myself because they thought they were safe in their stone fortress. Little did they know I have eyes on everything they care about and even have someone on the inside. As I watch them walk, observing every little detail of their movements, becoming a little too entranced by her curves. The way her hips swayed as she took each step. The way her clothing clung to her figure keeping, little to no secrets about what might be underneath.

Until they disappear out of view, and I turn away walking in the direction I had come until my gait picks up speed. Thrusting upward, lifting off the ground untethered from the earth, I ascend. Soaring through the air with my arms stretched wide, the breeze brushing my face, chilling me to the bone. I gaze down up down the deplorable city below. How I detest the city, this realm truly has a backward idea of civilization.

I begin to lower down as I grow closer to my destination, dipping down between the buildings I can hear the racket of the city growing closer. Some obnoxious people in the street, dogs barking, cars driving past at increasing speeds, and the worst sound of all; the wailing of a police sirens speeding down a nearby highway. I scoff at the sounds and modern ideas of culture.

Ducking down into an empty alleyway, landing firmly on the damp concrete. Pausing to look around checking no one is watching me. I approach the red brick building to my left. Behind a disgusting dumpster is an old metal door, motioning my hand with one motion I slide it over to reveal the entrance. Opening it with my hand grasping the cold brass knob and entering the hollow abandoned building.

The widows are yellowing and most of them are cracked. Some are covered with foggy white sheets of plastic. There are areas of the wall that are missing bricks and collapsing. Some walls are covered with moss and other foliage as Mother Nature is starting to take back the land that is rightfully hers.

I climb a flight of grated steps directly to the right of the doorway. Following them to the top until there is no longer any space to climb. Proceeding on the path, I turn right onto a catwalk, crossing through the doorway midway across into a glass gallery. This area is connected to a dark decaying hallway, I follow the hallway to an area with many doors across from one another. I slink past a few and enter the largest door at the end of the hall. Walking into a dark room filled with everything the modern world has afforded me, which isn't much.

Berlin DiVittore

    In a vacant studio apartment, the current place where I take up residency. It isn't much and I'd hardly call it home, but it is mine and most of all it is private. I take off my coat, hang it on the broken sconce to the right of the entrance, and close the door behind me.

    I scan the empty room, to the left of the entrance is an entire wall of tinted windows looking out into the orange and yellow lights of the city. On my right is a small writing desk and a ragged lamp, the only real source of light in the entire space. The right wall is covered with a trail of papers, photographs, and maps pinned to the wall. A derelict ruddy lazy boy sits waiting for me to rock and scheme as I fester staring at my wall of prejudice.

    Just across from that in the exact center of the room facing away from the entrance is my bed. Which is an old mattress propped up on and rickety oak bed frame. On either side at the head of the bed are wooden crates, temporarily being used as makeshift nightstands. At the foot of the bed is on tattered rectangular trunk. It has a padlock on it, but it is not clasped shut.

I continue past this area to the far-right corner of the room there is an old dining table set for one in the kitchenette area. This area is separate from the rest of the room with a long lime wash green countertop branching out of the wall. On the farthest wall on the small section of the counter, I see only my mini fridge, microwave, and hotplate. In the two short cupboards above are the few dinnerware and cutlery I could find on one side. On the other side are some cookware, and a whole shelf of herbs. Along the far-right wall is a chest freezer, nudging the lime counter.

I open the fridge and pull out a few items and I begin to prepare my meal. Then off to my left, I hear thumping footsteps approaching. Unalarmed I simply reach into the chest freezer and pull out a large sirloin steak. I drop it into a large rusty metal bowl with the name, 'SCAMP' printed on the side. I place the bowl on the floor not soon after my pet gymona approaches it.

With one breath she breaths fire on the meat just enough to melt the ice. She begins tearing at the raw flesh, as I continue to cook my meal. I sit at the table and eat my dinner quickly and with little fuss. I then place the dirty bowl in the plastic tote on the floor that sits just beneath a leaky faucet.

Leaving the kitchenette feeling full but hardly satisfied I sit in the armchair just to the left of my bed facing away from the windows. I pull my phone out of my pocket and begin to look at the social media page of Ashton Livingston. The one thing I did not loathe about this realm, is their ability of instant communication.

I see a photo of Jezebel, as she is called now, in a fairy costume. I save the photo to my device, print it out, and pin it on the wall with the other. Then I sit back down in my chair and stare at her. Her figure once more teases me with its curves. I could feel my cock getting hard just thinking about her.

Just at that moment, there is a knock at the door. I get up and open the door to find one of the only faces I can stand looking at these days.

"Hey Baby, I brought you some more groceries," Trixie says as she enters the room handing me a brown paper bag. Taking the bag from her I grin pleased not only by her presence but that she didn't come empty-handed.

I walk the bag over to the kitchen leaving the door wide open, as she finds a place to set down her purse and removes her coat. Then she follows me into the kitchen, her stilettos clicking on the floor as she walks. Setting the paper bag down on the counter I turn to grab her just as she enters the room. She squeals with delight as I fill my hand with her ass and kiss her forcefully. Then I lift her onto the counter, groping her as we kiss.

"You came just in time I was just starting to feel the urge for some pussy." I say with a sensual voice.

"Well, me-ow." She teases back with a little giggle.

"You have time for a fuck." I say bluntly, whilst our tongues become more tangled.

"Give it to me Baby." She says impatiently already tussling with my belt and unbuttoning my pants. Lifting her, I then walk her over to my bed, both our bodies tumbling on it. Removing our clothing hastily and without difficulty, I gaze upon her nakedness. Raise her legs, I hold them on either side of my body. Then without notice, I penetrate her with my dick.

Grunting as I drive my body deep into hers, her hands rubbing and groping her bosom. I watch as she arches her back in pleasure, her hands still full of her large breasts. I then release my hold on her legs and drop my body on the bed. Catching myself with my hands so I am hovering just above her. I continue to enter her pussy with my rock-hard cock, feeling the pressure beginning to build. She wraps me up with her arms and legs pulling me into her deeper. The bed creaks as we collide in sensual pleasure.

"Oh, Thaddy! Yes!" She cries out, I kiss her vigorously. Picking up speed as I feel the climax nearing, I begin to groan loudly with pleasure. Still thrusting I lift my head toward the entrance just as someone familiar steps into the doorway. This entices me further causing me to release my load.

She screams as we complete our task, removing my shuddering member from her body I grab a small blanket and cover her nudeness, before stepping off the bed and approaching my new visitor in the buff. This makes me feel powerful and in control.

"Hello Bastian, how did you find me?" I inquire.

"It was not hard, just followed the sounds of torture." He quips back unflinchingly. "Thad, please cover yourself. It's bad enough I had to witness you bedding that poor creature, but now I have to stare upon your nakedness." He says gesturing to the bed, as we both watch my naked conquest scamper off to the bathroom.

    I grab my pants from the crumpled pile on the floor and slip them on but leave them undone. Then I make my way to my lazy boy and sit as if on my throne, addressing my subject.

    "So, Bastian? Care to tell me the real way you have discovered my layer?" I pry, feeling frustrated my fortress of solitude had been revealed, and by my nemesis no less.

    "You think I didn't see you hiding amongst the shadow in the courtyard just now? Why else do you think I hastily escorted Jezebel inside?"

    "So, you saw me and followed me then?"

    "I will admit it was difficult, but I did have a little help." He began, and I grimaced, locking my jaw as he talked slowly, pacing as he spoke.

"I had begun to think you bested me and I had started my search too late. Granted it would have been worth it because I did get a long goodnight kiss from my sweet Jezebel. That is until I saw your girl, get out of a nearby vehicle and I just followed her. I did take a moment to have a look around, hope you do not mind?"

Then he pauses once more and picks up a ring that I keep by my bedside, looks it over briefly, and continues, "I see you were well occupied, so I took my time. Not too much time mind you, I know you never did have the same stamina as I do."

"I don't need stamina when my equipment has always been better." I snap, picking up his not-so-subtle jab at my sex drive. He says nothing, just glares at me, and continues the course of the conversation.

"So, what do you want Thad?"

"I told you I want Jezebel."

"Who is Jezebel?" I hear Trixie growl, coming up behind me. Now fully clothed as she exits the bathroom, Her auburn hair in a mess, lipstick smeared across her left cheek, and dark smudges under her eyes. "Is she the chick you have plastered all over your wall like some creepy stocker? I never thought much of it, thought you were like a Private Detective or something, but now I see you're just a creep!" She squeals before gathering her things, with no manner of hast. Then making her way out she stops and says, "I don't who she is, but she is better off without a bastard like you!"

Then she takes a moment to gawk at Sebastian who grins at her before her final exit. Hearing her shoes clicking down the hall, the sound fading as she became more and more distant.

"Women these days are more fun to play with but absolutely no class. You win some, you lose some I guess." I comment, trying to remove the awkward tension from the room having just been scolded in from of my nemesis.

"Well, you can't have her, she would never fall for your schemes," Sebastian says, ignoring my commentary and guiding the conversation once more back to the topic at hand.

"You forget, Briggita is a part of her." Then he chuckles, making me clench my fists in rage.

"That is why you were never given the Steorra Erestés coupling, you don't understand it. Jezebel is of her own mind. Her soul has been reborn, her emotions are different because she is different."

"Same beautiful body though," I interject into his monologue. Realizing this got a rise out of him as he scowled, I rise to my feet and begin stalking around the room slowly. I persist, "I bet you have bedded her already. You have tasted her delicious lips. Your eyes have gazed upon every forbidden curve of her body. You've caressed every inch of the same buttery skin that I have."

"Only she gave herself to me I willing." He jabbed with a deep roar.

"Oh, Briggita was willing. Do you think that night was the only time we had done the deed? We had been copulating for months. In closets, in the stables, even did it in your bed once or twice, just for kicks." I smirk reminiscing about a time long since passed. Then I'm reminded of the memory of the night it ended and resume with a growl, "Only that night she got an ear full about her *destiny* from her mother and decided she shouldn't be with me anymore. That our love didn't matter as long as you were around, and she had a duty to her coven."

"You would have doomed us all! And just for the sake of your petty vendetta!" Sebastian barks suddenly.

"It wasn't petty, you got the girl. I am eldest, I should at least have been King!" Stunned by my counter, Sebastian retreats. Then grins, shakes his head, and lets out a laugh.

"Oh, so the truth comes out. How long have you known that we are kin?"

"Since Vladis confessed it to me just before I drove a stake through his heart!" I roar with fury, basking in the pleasure of the vengeance I was getting. Not only from the memory of killing our father but admitting it to my brother.

"You killed our father?"

"With pleasure."

"He spared you, raised you and still you murdered him? Why?"

"I was never good enough for him!"

"No one was! I am his heir, and he almost destroyed me with his expectations!"

"Oh, is the *wittle-bitty-kingy-wingy* gonna cry?" I taunt, pushing aside his words, "You were still getting the girl. I could have at least gotten the crown."

"The *Steorra Erestés* are meant to rule hand-in-hand and unite the kingdoms, but you got in the way!"

"It had never been done! I never would be! Vampires and Witches were never meant to be as one."

"Coming from the hybrid himself," Sebastian spoke lashing me with his words. With that, I met my limit charging him with a leap over the bed. Tackling him to the ground. We roll across the floor, both of us jumping to our feet simultaneously. Standing in a crouched stance preparing for the other to strike.

"We were friends Thaddeus. Brothers. You betrayed me by stealing the girl I loved."

"That was the point."

"Did you even really love her?"

"Of course, I did. Who wouldn't love her?"

"So why destroy her life?"

"She *was* my life, my whole life, I didn't have anything else. My own mother didn't even want me."

"You can't know that."

"I can, I found her a few years after my exile. She admitted it to my face, that she would never have kept me because I shared kinship with a blood-thirsty demon."

"She was afraid of you?" Sebastian questioned, straightening his stance, looking confused.

"Yes, even though I have no vampire abilities, aside from my increased physical strength and curse of immortality," I state plainly, scoffing in disgust at my own wretched existence. He says nothing in return, just stands there with a stupid look of confusion still plastered on his face.

Then having had my fill of interaction for the night I take this as my opportunity to rid my layer of this unwanted pest. Charging him at full speed crashing into his midsection with full force sending him flying backwards. His body smashing through the window, the glass shattering upon impact. His body flailing through the air before it begins its descent as gravity took hold. Standing in the shattered opening, I watch him fall, eager to see my foe hit the pavement below.

Unexpectedly he suddenly turns to face the ground and with posthaste unfurrows his wings. He then soars upward taking flight and disappearing into the night. I scream into the dead air, hoping he is still within earshot.

"I will come for her Sebastian! She will be mine!" I scream, feeling the words scratch my throat as they depart my mouth.

Then I turn, recoiling into my layer, now soiled with the stench of my enemy. Knowing he will return, and when he does, I won't be here. I will never let him get the jump on me like that again. I will take everything he loves. His girl, his throne, and then his life.

Chapter 21
Sebastian

I LOOP AROUND THE BUILDING AFTER BEING shoved out a window, my shirt tattered and waving in the breeze as I fly. Then landing in the alley just outside the entrance I look around for my partner in crime. At first, all I can see is the garbage scattered about and the simmering dampness of the pavement. Then I see some steam coming from a manhole in the street. The alley smells rotten and moist, I grimace at the scent, covering my mouth and nose.

"I'm over here." I hear her voice whisper from the shadows. I look to find her crouching behind some wooden pallets that lean against the opposite building. As our eyes meet, I swiftly join her in the damp hovel.

I look upon her face, its familiar features triggering the moment when we struck a little deal that night in the club. Our surroundings melting away, everything around us changing to that familiar moment.

There he was standing across the club on the opposite balcony. Smirking at me, his arms spread open revealing his shirtless body beneath his brown leather trench coat. His hands grasping the metal railing of the balcony barrier. That is when I noticed it, the ring. There upon his right index finger was the gold sun ring with a ruby stone. I fumed just thinking about how this ring came to be in his possession. Just then Trixie approached me from behind, and twirls around leaning backwards against the railing to face me.

She places her hand on my shoulder and says, "Hey, it's no worries, honest. He is just a creep anyway. A handsome creep but still, creepy." Just then, I got the brilliant idea.

I turned to her and whispered. "Trix, you think you could do me a favor."

"I like the scheming look in your eye. Anything, but for a price."

"Name it."

"You have to give me a kiss. A real kiss."

"Done," I respond without hesitation thinking only of my rage. Then we returned to the private booth where she had been serving me. Sitting together in the booth, she nestled up close to me. Then she closed her eyes and waited, and I saw her lips slightly puck as she anticipated the kiss.

Readying myself, I closed my eyes and leaned in. Our lips touched and I felt her hands start to snake their way up my thighs. I stopped them with my hands, distracted by the tussle under the table I almost did not notice her trying to slip her tongue between my lips. With that I all at once broke away from her connection, sliding just slightly away in the booth.

"Oh, wowzah!" She said, curling her lips and fluffing her curly auburn hair. Then she grinned at me, "I'd say I got my monies worth, okay doll, what can do you for."

"I need you to seduce that man."

"The creepy one?" she said, appalled.

"Yes, just as a distraction, I need the ring he's wearing on his finger."

"Oh, so like a heist, you want me to theft for ya."

"No, I will do that, I just need you to be the bait and the distraction."

"So, you want me to use my womanly wiles." She said playfully intrigued, "I don't have to, you know?"

"No of course not, just befriend him, and when the time is right, we will perform our heist."

"Oh, I do love intrigue," she said with a flirtatious maniacal grin. Then she begins to giggle, her voice fading with an echo as the scenery shifts back to the damp alleyway where we sit, still crouching in our hovel.

"Did you get it?" She inquires, with anticipation.

"Yes," I say pulling out the ring that I had swiped during my discussion with Thad. It glistened in the street like dull gleam, the ruby sparkling with an enchanting red glow. "I said you didn't need to sleep with him."

"I know, but I've been getting kinda attached, he's actually kinda charming." She says her cheeks beaming with a subtle pink.

"Trix, you do not want to go there. Trust me, you deserve better than him. Now head on home before he catches you."

"Alright, Mr. Tall-Dark and Handsome." Then she kisses me on the cheek and scampers off to her car before speeding down the street.

Berlin DiVittore

I watch as she disappears into the urban jungle of concrete. Then I put the ring back in my pocket and take of back to the manor. I enter through the balcony doors of my bedroom. Upon entrance to find Jezebel sound asleep in my bed, where I left her.

I then walk into the foyer; the heat of the fire encompasses the room. It meets the chilled skin of my face with a burning sensation that quickly dissipates. I then take the ring out of my pocket, turn it over in my palm of few times, and then I grin having won the battle. Knowing the war has yet to be fought. I place the ring in the box on the mantle and sit on the sofa. Turning over all of Thaddeus's words in my head, they echoed inside me as I commence my strategizing whilst staring into the flames.

Chapter 22
Jezebel

STILL KIND OF GROGGY, I STRETCH AND yawn, enjoying the heat of the sun's rays. A part of me suddenly felt sad knowing Sebastian has never been able to bask in the sun's warm light. As I lay in bed enjoying some Vitamin D, stoking the sapphire amulet strung around my neck. I thought about the moment Sebastian gave it to me and how I challenged him to fit moon power into a smaller stone. Then suddenly I get an idea, jumping out of bed I throw on my robe and slippers and sneak out the door straight to the Sacred Study.

Berlin DiVittore

I run through the mansion as fast as I can after making it to the bookshelf,

I open the door that reveals the room behind it. Feeling a little nervous, still not used to being here on my own. Even still I have an idea and am not about to let it go to waste, I begin rifling through the books. I find all kinds of fun reading material, but nothing useful at the moment. Then I remember Sebastian's words, '*It is a protection amulet made from the same jewel as the crescent amulet of your ancestors. It is charged by moonlight and will protect you at all times I cannot'* his voice tapering off as my idea becomes more precise in my mind.

I walk across the room to a shelf filled with nothing but old leather journals. Then after flipping through a quarter of them, I found what I was looking for, I close it with a clapping sound, tuck it away tightly against my body, and make my way out. Then with one swish of my hand, all of the books I had removed glide back to their place on the shelf behind me.

I place the book in the drawer of the writing desk in my room and proceed to get dressed. Then I walk down to the dining room to see Ashton and Mama already dining with Sebastian.

"Well, good morning sleepy head." Mama chimes in her typical southern drawl. "I was beginning to think you were dead to the world." She teases with a smile but causing both Sebastian and Ashton to choke on their breakfast. Then after clearing their throats with a cough, they look up at each other from opposite ends of the table. I then find my seat, looking at Mama's confused reaction to her playful comment. Clearly growing suspicious of our behavior, having once again noticed someone choking on their meal.

"So, everyone slept well?" I query, changing the subject, attempting to distract her from the tension.

"Yes, I sleep quite well, I will say I do miss my honey, sleeping in the bed next to me."

"You mean Jezebel's father?" Ashton clarifies.

"Bless your heart, infidelity is not something we do in our family sugar." Mama quipped back with a southern smile, "We are as loyal as a hound dog." I smile and glance up from my plate to see Sebastian making loving eyes at me. I could feel the butterflies fluttering in my stomach and my cheeks getting warm.

"Jezebel, we better head out, or imma miss my flight Darlin'," Mama says interrupting my silent conversation with my handsome beau.

"You're right," I respond not breaking eye contact with Sebastian who was looking at me with a sideways cocky grin.

"Okay, ew you might as well just have sex on the table in front of us." Ashton jokes in disgust, "I've lost my appetite, I'll help with your bags, Ms. Jones." Ashton says getting up from the table and grabbing Mama's suitcase heading toward the door arm and arm.

"Ashton sugar, you can call me Lorraine." I hear Mama say as they disappear into the hallway. Their voices fade as they grow more and more distant.

"I have to take Mama to the airport and say my goodbyes. We will finish this when I return."

"I'll be waiting." He said temptingly. Then before I lose my wits I catch up to Ashton and Mama. We load up the trunk with all of Mama's bags and then we pile into Ashton's car as she speeds away from the manor.

"It was so wonderful having you visit Mama."

"I had a good time Darlin', I do so miss the comforts of home. I don't know how you can handle city life."

"I too am beginning to grow weary, but this is where I have found my people," I say, stoking my necklace as if it were a substitute for Sebastian's presence; and looking at

Ashton who is focusing on driving, trying her best to hide her smile.

We make it to the airport, and I help Mama check-in and find her bearings before giving her one final squeeze. I held her tightly, feeling her firm hold reciprocated. Then I gaze upon her face as if to capture every detail in my mind's eye. Unsure of the next moment I would gaze upon her face. Then before she could let go, I pull her in for one more tight squeeze.

"I love you, Mama," I say in a hushed tone, as if it were a secret.

"I love you too Baby girl!" She responds before releasing our hold on each other. A single tear rolls down my cheek, before I wipe it. Sniffling and taking a breath to regain my focus I smile.

"Safe travels. Text me when you home."

"I do you one better, I'll call you." Then I just smile soaking up the melodious tone in my mother's drawl.

Then she grabs her bag and wheels her suitcase behind her as she disappears in the chaos of San Francisco International Airport.

Then Ashton, who had been standing in silence off to the side, throws her arm around my waist in a sideways hug, I counter by draping my arm across her shoulders.

"Come on, let's go home," she says as we walk side by side, our arms intertwined around each other.

We drove into the parking garage and pulled into our regular space. Then getting out of the car we say our farewells.

"I will be back later to pick you up; I still don't think it's safe for you to sleep here."

"Got it. I'm just gonna check on the place and leave some money for the dog sitter. Maybe clean up a bit and grab a few things. Do you want me to get anything for you?"

"Oh, my laptop please."

"Done." She says before a quick hug.

Berlin DiVittore

We part ways as she makes her way toward the elevator, and I hop in my car. I drive to the manor thinking about the idea I had this morning, trying to distract myself from my new sudden loneliness. Pulling up to the gate of the manor to see it closed. Finding it a little curious that the gate was shut. I sat staring at it for a moment, noticing the 'SB' monogram for the first time. Then I roll down my window and flick my hand, causing the gate entrance to open. I drove up and parked just across from the front doors.

Walking up the stone steps of the manor, I ponder how to follow through with my marvelous idea. Not sure how to pull it off, having never performed magic like this before. Sure, it would take great skill.

Then I began to think about the Magi Vi ceremony Sebastian was telling me about to increase my power. Opening the door, excited to finally have the place to ourselves again, I enter the great hall, only to have my heart sink. I could almost hear it cracking at what I saw. There before me just on the bottom steps, a tall, beautiful woman was mounting my Sebastian. She had plump red lips, pale blue eyes, and long white hair draping down her slender perfect body.

She is wearing a peculiar outfit that exposes most of her whitish skin. He lay there beneath her, still fully clothed, pinned against the red carpet of the staircase. Looking at me standing in the doorway, our gaze meeting just as tears began to pool in my eyes.

"Jezebel!" He says, evidently surprised by my presence.

"Sebastian?" I respond softly, dropping everything I was holding as I felt my body become weak with devastation.

"It's not what you think..." He begins, before she cuts him off with a kiss, rendering him silent. Then the woman stands and begins strutting toward me with a conniving grin on her face.

Berlin DiVittore

"You must be Jezebel," she says in a seductive, haughty tone, "I'm Pandora Pollux."

THE END...*for now*

Fates

Krisi
(Krih-see)
Fate of Judgement

Anakyklono
(A-nah-ki-kloh-noh)
Fate of Reincarnation

Ponos
(Po-uu-noh-z)
Fate of Pain

Penthos
(Pehn-th-ohs)
Fate of Mourning

Parasma
(Pa-ruh-zmuh)
Fate of Passage

Name Pronuciation

Main Characters

Sebastion Baldovino SUH-BAS-CH-UHN | BALD-O-VEE-NO
Jezebel Jones JEZ-UH-BALL | JO-HN-Z
Ashton Livingston ASH-TUH-ON | LIH-VIHNGS-TUHN
Thaddeus Durrell TH-AH-D-EE-US | DER-RUH-EL
Lorraine Jones LUH-REH-A-IHN | JO-HN-Z
Jasper JAS-PER
Elisa UHL-IH-SUH
Pandora PAN-DOH-RAH | PUHL-EHKS

Side Characters

Malishca Sanballet MAL-EESH-KUH | SAN-BALL-EHT
Briggita Sanballet BREE-GEE-TAH | SAN-BALL-EHT
Antara Sanballet AN-TAHR-UH | SAN-BALL-EHT
Asmund Baldovino AS-MUH-ND | BALD-O-VEE-NO
Vladis Baldovino VLAH-DIS | BALD-O-VEE-NO
Patriva Baldovino PATR-EE-VA | BALD-O-VEE-NO
Angelina Baldovino AN-JIHL-EE-NHU | BALD-O-VEE-NO
Makenzie Durrell MEH-IH-KUHN-ZEE | DER-RUH-EL

Term Glossy

Ainigma- [Uh-nig-muh]

Term used to reference someone deem unfit by The Fates

Altar Room- [Oll-tr | Ru-m]

The main Chamber of the hidden Magic Corridor.

Familiar Spirit- [Fah-mil-lee-ar | Spear-it]

A supernatural entity, usually in the form of an animal, that is meant to aid and protect a witch on their journey."

Gýmona-[Gee-moh-nah]

Naked bear born in hellfire and perished by heavens waterfall.

Imperium- [Im-peir-ee-um]

Invasion/Control of the mind used by vampires

Incantas intrare-(In-Can-Tah-s |In-Tar-rea)

An incantation used to navigate the Porta Clavem

Term Glossy

Lingua scientia xéro omnia-
[Lin-guah | Scien-tia | zero | ohm-nee-ah]
To learn, read, and write in any/all languages

Magi Vi- [Man-gee | Vee]
The measure of one's magical Strength

Mensam- [Men-som]
Ritualistic Stone Table used to perform rituals and sacrifices

Omnicentennial Halo Moon-
[Ohm-ni-Suhn-teh-nee-uhl | Hay-Loh | Mu-N]
The name of the Celestial event that happens to the moon every one-hundred years

Omnicentennial Halo Ritual-
[Ohm-ni-Suhn-teh-nee-uhl | Hay-Loh | Ri-Choo-Uhl]
The name of the ceremony performed every one-Hundred years to join the Sapphire Vampire Clan and the Ruby Witch Coven

Term Glossy

Pente Stadia Thanatos-
(Pen-tah | Stay-Dee-ah | Than-Ah-Tos)
The five stages of death that rule judgement over all supernatural beings at the end of their Twenty-fifth year.

Porta Clavem- [Por-tah | Cla-v-um]
Portal Key

Sacred Study- [Say-kruh-d | Stuh-dee]
The library section of the Hidden Magic Corridor.

Steorra Erestés- [Steh-or-rah | Ehr-es-teh-s]
Star Lovers: The name used to reference the coupling made during the Omnicentennial Halo Ritual.

Thearapevo- [Thair-ah-peev-oh]
A healing spell

Ventus- wind

Translation Guide

Spanish
Fracaso sin esperanza
"...hopeless failure"

"Nunca podrías estar desesperado mi amor"
"You could never be hopeless, my love."

Italian
"Faremo sesso piu tardi, bellissimo"
"We'll have sex later, beautiful"

Frech
"Je vais me nourrir de toi aussi."
"I will feed on you also."

German
"Verstehen"
"Understand"

COMING FALL 2025

Will Jezebel be able to handle this heartbreak? Or will is it send her spiraling? Or has she become someone different since her last heartbreak? Even more, what does this mean for the Steorra Erestés? Who is this new stranger, and will she threaten Jezebels relationship with Sebastian? Will Thad finally have a chance to win her over? Or will Sebastian and Jezebels new deepened love save their relationship.

So many questions and more to come in the next addition to the "CRAVE SAGA" series by Berlin DiVittore.

About the Author

Berlin DiVittore is a Published, Freelance Writer and Illustrator who helps readers to escape the mundane burdens of everyday life. DiVittore has always know that she wanted to be a writer, and began writing at a very young age. She has published several poems and sketches in her local community college magazine; and even competed in speech/poetry competitions winning various medals and accolades.

After getting married and moving to Italy with her military husband, DiVittore began her journey to follow her dream and composed literary works of art. Her hope is to have a successful career publishing novels and children's books. DiVittore currently reside in the land of the midnight son, Alaska, with her family. Aside from writing, in her spare time DiVittore enjoys various activities beyond spending time with her family. DiVittore grew up in a small town in Nebraska, with her large.

DiVittore is available for writing projects, as well as private commissions. You can reach Berlin DiVittore at
bdivi.authorartist@gmail.com
or visit her website at

www.BDiVittore.com

www.ingramcontent.com/pod-product-compliance
Lightning Source LLC
LaVergne TN
LVHW091658070526
838199LV00050B/2203